Georgie's Beau

by

Shara Azod

This is a work of fiction. Names, characters, places, and incidents are products of the author's imagination or are used fictitiously and are not to be construed as real. Any resemblance to actual events, locales, organizations, or persons, living or dead, is entirely coincidental.

Copyright© 2009 Shara Azod
Editor: Lacynda Hill
Cover Artist: Shara Azod

All rights reserved. No part of this book may be used or reproduced electronically or in print without written permission, except in the case of brief quotations embodied in reviews. This is a work of fiction. All references to real places, people, or events are coincidental, and if not coincidental, are used fictitiously. All trademarks, service marks, registered trademarks, and registered service marks are the property of their respective owners and are used herein for identification purposes only. eBooks are NOT transferable. Re-selling, sharing or giving eBooks is a copyright infringement.

Note to ePirates and Those Who Use ePirate Sites:

Even if you did not personally put this book up to be pirated you are participating in a crime. Theft of intellectual property is still theft – a federal crime under U.S. law. But you probably don't care about that. Nor do you care about the money and effort it takes to produce an ebook. Authors of ebooks get paid based on the amount of books sold, as do a lot of editors and cover artists. We do not get cash upfront like New York authors; we don't receive advances for our work. Most of us have full time jobs while we work on the craft we love. You are stealing from us, our families and the people who depend on us for payment for their editing, art, or proofreading time. I would rather you didn't read anything I wrote at all. I don't need readers like you. I don't wish any ill will on you, I just wish you would go away and let the people who enjoy me enough to pay for my work do that.

Thanks for shopping with us.
Kindest Regards, Customer Care

RETURNING GOODS

Please re-pack, in the original packaging if possible, and send back to us at the address below. **Caution!** Don't cover up the barcode (on original packaging) as it helps us to process your return.

We will email you when we have processed your return.

---✂--

PLEASE complete and include this section with your goods.

Your Name: _____

Your Order Number _____

Reason for return _____

Select: Refund my order ☐   Replace my order ☐

(Please note, if we are unable to replace the item it will be refunded.)

Return to:

---✂--

```
RETURNS
Unit 22, Horcott Industrial Estate
Horcott Road
FAIRFORD
GL7 4BX
```

Chapter One

Blakely, GA

Late 1930s

"Come on, Georgie. Dance with me."

Beau Dupuis was one seriously fine man. His devilish baby blues twinkled at her as she dodged his seeking hands without dropping a glass from her overburdened tray. His black hair gleamed in the dim light, one lock falling into his left eye. As much as Georgina's hand itched to push it back she knew that would just invite trouble. There were already plenty of nasty stares aimed in Beau's direction already tonight. He was taking a serious chance spending so much time at the local jook joint; and not because he was white either. Times were hard, and his daddy owned just about everything in town. People always looked for trouble when troubles were heavy on them. It was a way to blow off steam and blame somebody else for all that was wrong in their lives.

It was funny that so many claimed not to hold with race mixing, when all around you the various shades and textures of the people of the deep South declared otherwise. She could think quite of few children running around the small town of Blakely that clearly had a little cream in their coffee. It was not something that was talked about, it just was. And for those who dared to break the color line, the consequences were sometimes too much to bear.

"I'm working, Mr. Dupuis," she informed him, scurrying around the bar before he could touch her.

It was bad enough her father ran a juke joint; that fact alone assured she would never be welcome around "decent folk." Her mother had been a half-Indian and half-black, never bothering to marry her father before having his child and promptly dying. Despite the fact that her skin was the color of dark, rich, molasses, most folks considered her a red skin breed. It never made much sense to her, the prejudice against Indians who were here long before anybody else. She guessed everybody needed somebody to look down on, if only to make themselves feel a little better about their lot in life.

Any chance she had of ever getting married and settling down was with the customers they had, and Beau wasn't one of the prospects. He wasn't just white, he was the son of the mayor, who just happened to also be the richest plantation owner in all of Early County. While so many planters were going bust and moving on into bigger cities, Branford Jefferson Dupuis prospered. Most of the men here tonight either worked in his canning factory, in his fields, or in his peach orchards. Their family owned half of the town. Not many folks around here had much of a choice were they worked. With so many of the white farmers who owned smaller tracts of land having moved on, the Dupuis Plantation was just about the only gainful employment here 'bouts. That meant Beau, the heir apparent, could go just about anywhere he pleased. Even a backwoods colored juke joint. Only an idiot would gainsay him.

That didn't mean it was okay for Georgiana to be messing around with him. Black girls had to be very careful who they were seen talking to. Fooling around with the wrong man meant being ostracized by most and a reputation that often led to far, far worse than someone not talking to you. She wasn't about to become one of the fallen. Those kinds of women were seen as only good for a quick roll in the hay. Many times one of the poor souls considered "loose" or white men's whores were found in the fields raped and battered almost beyond recognition. It didn't seem to matter that some of those women never had a choice. Georgiana was in a precarious position; she didn't have too many options, but she would be damned if someone took away the few she had.

Sounded simple enough, if only Beau didn't make her hands sweat and her heart just about beat right out of her chest every time she saw him. Lord above, the man did something to her. Whenever he turned those beautiful eyes her way she could feel heat suffuse her face and her nipples became harder than rocks. There was something about him. Maybe it was the way he looked at her like she was the only woman in the world. Or it could be that slow lazy smile that went perfectly with that slow lazy drawl. Whatever it was, the man moved her in ways no other had ever done. She fought the attraction tooth and nail, but it was always there right under the surface. And he knew it, damn his eyes.

"Why are you so mean to me sweet Georgie, mine?" Beau whined, leaning over the bar. At least she told herself it was whining. That deep, sexy drawl gave her goose bumps inside as well as out.

"I'm not your anything, Beau Cantwell Dupuis," Georgina replied tartly, one eye on him and another looking around at who might be listening. "And you best hurry and finish your drink and get on home. We're fixin' to close up for the night."

Sunday nights were never very crowded. Sunday dinners were still big, even if there wasn't much on the table these days. Most folks were home with their families after spending most of the day at church, talking and laughing, and just enjoying being together. Georgina's father refused to go to church, though he had never stopped her. She had stopped herself after it became clear she would never be welcomed in the House of God. If that wasn't a kick in the pants she didn't know what was.

"Go on if you want to, Georgie-girl," her father had said. "Nothin' there but a bunch of busybody know-it-alls, every bit as much a sinner as me. Difference is I don't pretend to be no better than anybody."

He had been right. The women had smiled in her face, but talked about her like a dog when her back was turned. Not a one of the girls her age would talk to her, much less sit with her. The good men of the church gave her the cold shoulder in front of the good church ladies, but tried to get her in the woods when they thought nobody was looking. No one ever invited her home to dinner, though most strangers just passing through got all kinds of invitations. It just wasn't worth the effort.

"Alright, everybody," James Willard called from the front near the makeshift stage. "Time to go. Most of y'all got to get up early anyway."

There were a few grumbles, but the patrons obediently trudged out of the small shack towards wherever they called home. A couple of men had cars and gave several others a ride back into town, but most left on foot. All except for Beau.

"Why are you still here?" Georgiana demanded.

Beau shrugged giving her a heart-stopping grin. "To help you clean up," he offered, rising from the wooden bar stool to round the bar where she stood.

Georgiana looked around for her father; only to realize he was probably walking around outside, ensuring everyone had left. He did that every night, as Beau would know. He had been here most nights for the past month or so. She took a step back as he approached, finding herself trapped between him and the wall.

"Look, Beau, I think you better leave."

Her voice trembled slightly, lowering to almost a whisper. She was no fool; she knew what he wanted. Even though she knew she should be horrified at the situation, she found her heart racing with excitement. It was forbidden. Completely outside the unwritten law. But she wasn't afraid. Lord help her, she was excited. Leaning forward, he braced his hands on the wall trapping her in a cage of his arms.

"Now Georgie, tell me. Why are you so mean to me?"

Beau had the most beautiful voice. All deep and slow like homemade syrup. It went well with his almost angelic face. Her eyes darted from his face to his lips. They were full and luscious, bringing to mind soft kisses stolen under a moss-covered pine. And they were getting closer.

"I'm not mean to you, Mr. Dupuis."

"My name is Beau," he chided, moving one hand to caress her cheek. "Say it for me, sweetheart."

Oh, God he was going to kiss her! She knew it just as sure as she knew her name. And she was going to let him.

"B-Beau," she managed, just before his mouth touched her own.

His lips swept down on hers, not soft and gentle as she always imagined her first kiss would be, but possessive and forceful. He angled his head, his tongue snaking out to lick her bottom lip, causing her to moan. Taking advantage, he thrust his tongue into her mouth, tasting all she had to offer. Before she knew what was happening, his arms gathered her closer, lifting her off her feet. Her back was pressed tightly against the wall, as he pushed his body against hers. Georgiana gasped as she felt something hard press against the apex of her thighs. Her head spun at new and unexpected sensations engulfing her. She felt hot and achy, like she had fever. She tingled in places she never had before, wanting something so desperately, but she had no idea what it was.

Beau reached down to place her leg around his waist. She let him gratefully, wrapping the other leg around him as well. Oh, sweet heaven she was in need so badly she thought she would die of it. When he rocked the hard bulge between his legs against her privates she almost cried out in joy. Yes, oh Lord, yes! Just a little bit more!

"That's it, baby. Feel how bad I want you," he whispered, tearing his mouth away from hers.

Georgiana could do little more than whimper as he rocked against her ruthlessly. Her entire world felt like it was tilting, spinning out of control. She felt her body climbing higher and higher. She was sure she was about to die, but she didn't want him to stop.

"Look at me Georgie," Beau demanded harshly. "Let me see it, baby."

See what, she didn't know.

All of a sudden her body seized, tightening then exploding into pieces. Her mouth opened in a soundless scream as her eyes flew to his.

"Oh, God! Oh, my God," she gasped, hanging on to him for dear life.

"Yeah, Georgie, baby. Just like that."

He lips took hers once again, capturing the loud moans as she exploded again and again, each shockwave more intense than the last. Finally, after what seemed like hours, she gradually relaxed, closing her eyes in the warm afterglow.

She was not naïve enough to believe she had just given him her virginity, but she knew whatever he had done to her was damned close to going all the way. And she had loved every minute of it.

Beau let her slide to her feet, holding on to her as she caught her balance. This could not happen again. She had come within a hair of ruining any chance of a future outside running a backwoods juke joint. She wanted a family, a home, and some children. Being a white man's mistress was not going to get any of that for her.

"Are you okay, Georgie?"

Snapping her attention back to the man in front of her, she nodded briskly.

"I-I don't pretend to know what just happened, but Beau, it can never happen again."

Beau's eyes narrowed at her, his blue eyes turning dark and stormy. Georgina shivered, as if caught in an actual squall, but she couldn't back down.

"I mean it, Beau. I plan to get married someday, and I can't…let you have your way with me. What decent man would want me then?"

He was so quiet, so still, for a moment she was afraid of what he might do. Not that she thought he'd hurt her, but she knew she would be helpless to resist if he decided to force the issue. Closing her eyes, she willed with all her might that he would understand. After a few moments, she felt his hand caress her cheek.

"What man wouldn't want you? Decent or otherwise," he finally answered softly before turning and walking away.

Georgiana slumped against the wall as she watched him go. *Nothing good can come of it*, she kept reminding herself to keep from calling him back.

By the time her father returned, she had cleaned the tables, stacking the chair on top, swept the floor, and was just about finished washing the Mason jars they used for glasses. She didn't look up as she heard him approach; she was sure he would see what she had done all over her face. Not that he would disapprove. She wasn't exactly sure what her father would think.

"Saw the Dupuis boy, leavin'," James informed her, like she didn't already know. "Looked to be in a sorry state."

"Why is that?" she dared to ask without looking up. Her father saw far too much.

"'Spect you would know better than most. Seems some gal got that boy's nose wide open."

Her eyes flew to her father's face. He stood beside her calmly drying the glasses she had washed like it was any other night. Did he know what they had done? He gave no sign of being upset, but then, in her twenty years she had rarely seen her father upset.

"Daddy, why don't you just go ahead on and say whatever it is you're thinking?"

But she was afraid she knew already. He never thought too much of propriety. He lived his life as he saw fit. He never understood his daughter's need to fit in. She was tired of being on the outside looking in. Was that really so bad?

"Ain't saying nothing," James replied evenly without pausing in his task. "Y'all will figure it out. Sooner rather than later to hear the boy tell it." Carefully folding the drying towel, James turned to leave. Just before he made it to the side room where he slept, he paused and looked back. "You know, Georgie, sometimes the things we want ain't always what we need. Living your life for others ain't no way to be happy. How many of those people you think so much about are really happy, gal? You think about that long and hard before you go doing something you can't take back."

Georgiana watched him go, struggling to hold back the tears that threatened to fall. He hadn't said anything that hadn't been in the back of her subconscious, but it hurt to hear it. Her quest for respectability hurt him, she knew. She wished she could just make him understand. This wasn't about rejecting him or anything he stood for. She was so very lonely. He gave her the very best he had, imparted what wisdom he could, but nothing could make up for the loneliness she felt in her very bones. She had never really had a friend, never really talked to much of anybody except the people that came to the juke. They were friendly to a point, but he couldn't make up for her lack of friends her own age. Maybe her father just didn't understand, but she needed to be close to someone other than her father.

*****

Beau leaned his head against his Convertible Cabriolet. He took in huge gulps of air trying to calm down enough to drive home. Every fiber of his being screamed for him to go back inside and finish what he started, but he wouldn't do that. He had to give her time to adjust. He would make her his; tonight was just not the time. He forced the issue, she was liable to up and run away. It was going to be hard enough to court the obstinate woman; he didn't want to have to chase her cross-country to do it.

He drove back to the plantation without really seeing where he was going. He hadn't meant to scare Georgiana, but he knew he had. It drove him crazy the way she tried to ignore the pull between them. He couldn't be in the same room with her without getting rock hard. Hell, it seemed his damn prick would only work when she was around. He hadn't meant to touch her. He swore to himself he would take it slow. But that woman drove him out of his head.

He knew her objections. It wasn't like they could run off to the nearest preacher and get married. There were laws against that. Nor was he planning on keeping her as a mistress. He would never disrespect her like that. If he were honest, he would have to admit he had no idea what he was planning on doing. He just knew he couldn't see the rest of his life without Georgiana Mae Willard by his side. It would mean leaving Blakely, but he didn't care.

For the last year, he had been unable to do little more than watch her from afar as she smiled sweetly and kept him and everyone else at arm's length. That smile of hers never quite reached her eyes though. It broke his heart to see her look so lost and lonely. He wanted to beat the whole damn town to a bloody pulp about the way they treated her. The uppity church ladies who held their noses up in the air when she walked by weren't fit to kiss her dainty little feet. His heart fell to pieces every time he saw the pain she tried so hard to hide when she thought no one was looking.

He was looking. He was always looking.

He would give anything to just once see a smile reach her eyes. To hear her laugh out loud like she didn't have a care in the world. Life was hard enough without having to carry somebody else's baggage. If only he could make her see that.

"Been out to that damn place again?"

Beau hadn't noticed his father as he got out of his car and made his way up the wide steps to the house. The old man had been sitting in a rocker in the corner, smoking a cigarette. No doubt, he was just waiting to slink off to Ida's. Either that or he had just slunk back home. Given it was still early, it was more likely he was going rather than coming.

"Yes, sir," Beau replied hoping to get this over with. He was still sporting a raging hard on. He could still taste Georgie's sweet tongue. One day soon, he would taste all of her. Just the thought made his eyes cross and a moan well up from his gut. He managed to swallow it before his father caught wind of the direction of his thoughts. The last thing he needed tonight was a lecture from the king of hypocrisy.

To Beau's surprise, his father said nothing, nodding for him to enter the house. Before he could open the door, his father's voice stopped him once more.

"You're a man now, Beau. I expect you to act accordingly."

His hands clinched the doorknob so hard his knuckles were white. Act accordingly? Like fucking the housekeeper while your wife was either drunk or passed out on laudanum? No matter how badly he wanted to say it out loud, he couldn't. One didn't call Branford Dupuis on his bullshit, no matter how deep it was. That, and all he wanted to do was go inside to bed.

"Saw James Willard's gal in town the other day. No wonder you spend so much time out there in the woods. When you're ready, I got a place on the far side of the property. We need someone to help Ida out anyway."

Beau's blood ran ice cold before heating to the point of boiling. He walked with leaden feet into the darkened interior of his parent's home, closing the door softly behind him. His father's words stabbed straight into his heart.

Was this the life he was bound and determined to bring to Georgie? Was he damning her to a life of some kind of sexual bondage? Bitter bile filled his mouth as he drug himself up the winding staircase to his room. That's exactly what he was doing. And the bitch of it was, there wasn't a soul who would try to stop him. She had tried to tell him that tonight, but he had refused to listen.

He was no better than his father.

"I won't do it to her," he declared to his empty bedroom.

There may have been no one but the ghosts of his ancestors to hear him, but it felt better to say it out loud.

"I will not sentence her to that kind of life."

The cold, empty night air mocked him. Even as he said the words, he knew he was lying to himself.

Chapter Two

Sweat trickled down between the valley of Georgie's breasts, making her itch unbearably. It may be well into September, but autumn showed no signs of making itself known. It wasn't yet ten o'clock and the sun was beating down relentlessly. The muggy air weighed her down as she scrubbed the week's laundry. Her father used to take it into town, but lately he had been hinting that maybe she would be more useful around the house rather than working in the juke. She had tried to do both, but it was just too damn wearing.

She knew what this was all about. Her father set out to make her do all the things she would be doing as a wife, thinking it would cure her of her desire to be married so badly. He wanted to show her what a life of dreary work, night and day, would be like. He had even talked about getting some chickens and maybe a cow for fresh milk.

To make matters worse, she had seen neither hide nor hair of Beau Dupuis for over three weeks. Not since that night…

Sighing, Georgie lifted the basket of wet clothes and lumbered to the recently hung clothesline. It was barely ten in morning, but the sun was pounding down unmercifully. She decided to do the laundry and various other chores in her slip and nothing else. There was no one around this early so it wasn't like she was in any danger of being seen. It was one of the pluses of living out in the country away from almost everybody. The weather was far too heavy for many clothes. Her father was still in bed, sure to not be up until well after noon. Saturday nights were always wild and ruckus. She had helped out as much as she could, but she wasn't able to stay awake very long. Just long enough to see Beau wasn't going to be making an appearance.

Despite the thousand and one lectures she had given herself, she missed Beau like she missed a piece of herself. It made no sense because she really didn't know him all that well, but she felt his absence around the club at night. She tried to get him out of her head, but he was last thing she saw before she drifted off to sleep, and he was the star attraction in her dreams. She was really beginning to regret trying to push him away, no matter how much she knew it was the best thing for her.

"It's for the best," she sighed to herself out loud. "Nothing good could ever come of it."

"Come of what?"

Georgie almost jumped out of her skin. She didn't have to turn around to see who had spoken. He may have snuck up on her, but he was sure as hell making himself known now. She couldn't move even if she wanted to; and as he pressed his body against her back, she knew she didn't want to. Her body melted back into his without thought.

"Were you thinking about me again, Georgie-mine?" Beau gave her a wicked smile; a smile that promised a trip straight to hell and guaranteeing she would enjoy the ride.

Georgie shivered at the soft words drawled in her ear, every bit as much as the strong arms brushing the underside of her breast as he reached up to help her pin the clothes to the line.

"I don't think about you at all, Beau Dupuis." The lie felt good to say, though she knew he probably wouldn't swallow it.

Her voice was all breathless and needy, giving voice to things she dared not admit — even to herself. She was going to move away. Just one more minute.

"I thought about you, sweetheart." He tugged on her ear gently with his teeth. "Every second of every day."

She whimpered as his hands moved to caress her belly, his tongue snaking out to lick a bead of sweat traveling from her neck to her collarbone. She held on to the clothesline for dear life as she felt him moving behind her. His erection pushed against the soft cushions of her buttocks, rocking her softly.

"Beau, please!" she pleaded.

Already the tension was damn near unbearable and he hadn't done much. Just the feel of his skin against her own, the heat of his body pressed so close to her. It was enough to make a girl want to cry.

The sultry breeze caressed her thighs as he pulled up her slip almost casually. One hand had moved up to lightly skim her chest, causing her to moan as she moved restlessly against him. She cried out when she felt one wondrously thick finger slide against her wetness.

"Oh, naughty little Georgie," he rasped. "You're not wearing any panties."

She wanted to tell him it was only because it was so hot, but she couldn't. His finger had begun to probe and pry at her unexplored sex, while his wicked thumb traced lingering circles around her exposed nubbin. The hand that had previously skimmed her breast so tentatively became aggressive, kneading and pinching first one and then the other, only to start all over again. She felt her eyes roll into the back of her head when one finger entered her, pressing inside, thrusting, seeking. Her breath came out in pants as she gave herself over to the mastery of his hands. Her skin was suddenly much too tight; everything within her threatened to burst free. One mighty thrust and he was hitting a spot she never knew existed. Colors swam before her eyes, her knees threatened to buckle.

"Oh, God, Beau I can't...I can't," she panted, knowing her heart would give out at any minute.

"Yes, you can, sugar. Just let go. Let go for me."

As if her body needed permission, she burst apart at his soft-spoken command. Birds flew startled from the trees at her sobbing cry.

Beau hurt. His cock pressed painfully against the crotch of his pants, threatening to burst the seams. His body pulsated with desperate need, a need to bury himself deep inside of her. He hadn't meant to touch her. He had only wanted to see, her. To ensure himself that she was alright and far better off without him disturbing her peace. The sight of her looking so sad and alone had damn near made him cry. In his way of thinking, Georgie should never look forlorn or lonely. She should be wreathed in smiles, pampered, and catered to. He didn't like to see her doing backbreaking labor.

He should have walked away. But when she had stood to hang the wash… He had moved to her before considering the implications. Before he knew it, his arms were around the one thing he wanted more than he had ever wanted anything before. She felt so unbelievably good in his arms. So right. Good intentions flew right out the window as soon as he heard her sigh of acceptance. Nothing on earth could be sweeter than the feel of her body melting into his own.

He needed this woman like he needed his next breath. He had tried to stay away. He had tried so hard to stay away. Tried with everything within him to just leave her alone and let her live her life. But the mere thought of her being with anyone else, smiling at anyone else, God help him, lying with anyone else, drove him to the brink.

"Come with me, Georgie," he rasped desperately. "Please, come with me now."

The slight nod of her head was all he needed before he swept her up into his arms, depositing her in his car before she could change her mind. He didn't think as he drove as if the devil was after him. Perhaps he was. In the back of his mind, he knew what he was doing would change her life forever, but he just couldn't let go. She may hate him for the rest of her life afterwards, but living the rest of his days never knowing, never touching just once, it was more than he was willing to do. He had to know. He had to touch, to taste, to feel.

Before he knew where he was going, he pulled up to the very house his father had pointedly mentioned in passing not so long ago. Funny, he didn't feel quite so sick to his stomach anymore. Perhaps he was the one that was the hypocrite. The thought shocked him right out of the haze of need that had wrapped so tightly around him just a few seconds ago. His eyes traveled down the red clay road not really seeing much of anything.

"Georgie, I can take you back home right now if that's what you want me to do," Beau sighed, defeated.

It was the right thing to do. But he had known that before he brought her here. Hell, he had known that before ever driving out to her place. It was seeing this damn house, all recently white washed with the shutters painted dark green. The recent and obvious updates to the exterior made him wander just how long his father had been observing him. It wasn't a shack, he'd give his father that much. Not a shotgun house either. There was a large kitchen, two bathrooms complete with indoor plumbing, three full-sized bedrooms, and even a walk-in pantry. All the windows had been replaced and cleaned. Beau didn't doubt for a second that the interior would be fully furnished. The kitchen might even be stocked with food. He didn't know who disgusted him the most at that moment; his father or himself.

"I don't want to go back home, Beau."

The soft declaration made him turn to face her. So perfect, with those liquid, brown eyes staring right through to his soul. Her smooth, dark skin set off the pristine white of the slip she was almost wearing. Damn, he hadn't even thought to let her get dressed. Just snagged her up and drove pell-mell down the road. Anybody could have seen them. It was a true Godsend most folks were in church. Thank goodness they hadn't had to pass one.

"Honey, you know what going into this house is gonna mean, don't you?"

He had to ask. She needed to be sure. It wasn't that long ago she declared she was aiming to get married, not play the whore for some spoiled white man. She hadn't actually said that much, but the sentiment had been right there spelled out for him in black and white—literally.

Georgie sighed and looked away. Yes, she knew what it would mean. She also finally understood what her father had been trying to tell her without words. She could get married and settle down. Start a family. But she wouldn't be happy, and she would never be considered "acceptable" to all those she had tried so desperately to appease. Her choices may not be many, but they were stark. If she wanted to stay here in the only place she had ever called home, there were only three options. She could die a spinster, living with her father and carrying on his business after he was gone, she could marry some sharecropper, field hand, or blues singer—nobody else would have her given her family history—or she could find a man like Beau.

Had she not been so powerfully attracted to him, there would be no choice to make. She would marry the first man who asked just so she wouldn't be alone. It was rolling the dice and the odds weren't in her favor, but she knew she would do it.

But she was attracted to Beau. She felt his loneliness, his need, as deeply as she did her own. She didn't know if it was going to work. She didn't know if she even wanted it to. She did know she wanted this right now. Tomorrow wasn't promised to anyone, she wanted take what joy she could find right now.

"I know what it means, and I'd be lying if I said I didn't care, but I have never wanted anything more than you right now."

No sooner than the words left her mouth, Beau was out of the car, yanking the passenger's side door open, and hauling her into the house. He didn't break stride until they were in the front bedroom and he was placing her in the center of the raised, four-poster oak bed.

"Tell me it's alright, Georgie," Beau murmured as he buried his head between her breasts. "Tell me you won't hate me for this later."

Georgie couldn't tell him anything at all; she was holding her breath as one big callus roughened hand slid up the side of her leg, taking her slip with it. The lips that made her drunk with burning need placed biting kisses along her collarbone, moving upward like he had all the time in the world. She wanted those lips on hers, if just to help her get some air. She felt the same burning ache he had ignited the night at the juke when he pinned her against the wall. It started in the pit of her belly, spreading like a July wildfire straight to her very core, making her panties grow damp and her nipples pebble. What was he doing to her?

"Lift up a sec, sweetheart," Beau murmured against her ear, pulling her up and sliding the slip over her head in one fluid motion.

He was kneeling over her, looking down as she flopped back on the soft mattress, his blues eyes darkening until they almost looked black. Georgie brought her arms up to cross her chest in a moment of shy embarrassment. No one had ever seen her naked, not since she was a small child. Beau captured her wrists, bringing them over her head so he could look his fill. She was too conscious of the plain, white, cotton underwear she had on. He was probably used to silks and satins, commodities George couldn't even dream about owning.

"Damn, Georgie-girl, you are beautiful!"

Her eyes snapped up to his at the soft exclamation. She was passably pretty she supposed, but beautiful? No one had ever called her such before. And the way he was looking at her now; how could such a fierce look make her feel so wanted?

When he covered her body with his own, she opened her arms with no resistance. If she lived a thousand years, she knew she would never find another human being on earth that made her feel the way Beau was making her feel right now. So wanted, so desirable. His acceptance was complete, without reservation. She almost cried from the sense of completeness.

His clothes were rough against her soft skin, but she didn't care. She loved the contrast rubbing against her, heightening every sensation. Her legs opened of their own accord, allowing him to settle against her questing mound. He rocked against her in leisurely strokes, his mouth traveling to seize one sensitive nipple after another. He was relentless, suckling, nipping, licking. Georgie gasped as tension built unbearably at her center, like water skins about to burst. It was so much more than the night at her father's juke, yet it wasn't enough.

"Beau, please," she gasped, not sure she wanted to experience what she knew was just over the horizon.

"It's okay, baby," he soothed, never pausing in his worship of her breasts. "Just relax and let go."

As if her body merely waited for his permission, she flew apart, crying out softly as she rode the tidal wave of her orgasm. She was unaware Beau had moved until she felt a slight breeze against the bare flesh of her vagina. Before she had a chance to protest, she felt something warm, wet and entirely too wickedly delicious take a languid stroke. She wanted to protest, but her words caught in her throat, making her unable to do anything more than struggle for breath and clutch hopelessly at his head.

Beau had died and gone to heaven. Georgie was the perfect combination of innocent and wanton; her responses so open and honest. He loved the way her skin heated at his touch, the way she gasped into his mouth as he gently stroked her. And, God, her taste! The sweetest Georgia peach never tasted as fresh or so sweet. He couldn't get enough. He lapped, slurped, and prodded, drinking every drop. He drove her over the edge again and again, somehow managing to rid himself of the confining clothes in his way.

He had to feel her against his bare skin. He needed to be inside this woman more than he had ever needed anything. He didn't understand this urgency driving him, but he knew he had to brand her, to make her his irrevocably, forever. He waited as long as he could, his engorged cock throbbing painfully, as if it were begging for the one thing they knew it needed. Georgie. His Georgie.

After bringing her over one last time, he trailed kisses against her velvety soft chestnut skin. The contrast between her mysterious darkness and his light tan drove him wild. It was beyond beautiful, it was the most erotic thing he had ever seen. Gathering her legs around his waist, he kissed her deeply, sharing her exquisite taste with her, loving how she opened without pause, not turning her head or keeping her lips tightly closed, but accepted his tongue without demur.

"Open your eyes, Georgie," he commanded, poised right where he needed to be.

As soon as she complied, he thrust inside her to the hilt, catching her gasp of pain in a devouring kiss.

Georgie had not been expecting the burning, tearing pain as Beau surged inside her. She tried to buck his body off of her, but he wouldn't be moved.

"*Shhh*, sweetheart, just relax," he soothed, raining tiny kisses all over her face. "I promise, baby, just relax. I'll make it good for you, I promise."

She didn't believe him, but as she took hold of her body, she noticed that the pain was receding. In its place, she felt an overwhelming sense of fullness. In fact, she could feel herself moistening as the burning turned into something else, an intense itch, and a yearning that she couldn't control. Georgie squirmed and moved her hips, exploring the delicious sensation.

The exquisite friction was incredible! Each parry and thrust seemed to stroke some inner fire higher and higher. She found herself moving with him, following his movements so as not to lose that excruciatingly heady feeling. She needed him closer, deeper. She couldn't get close enough!

"Beau, please!"

She had no idea what she was begging for, but she knew she needed something, and she needed him to give it to her.

Beau's unhurried, measured strokes intensified, increasing in force and coming faster. He had to grit his teeth in supreme effort not to blow. Lord, she was so amazingly tight, so wonderfully wet! He was determined to bring her with him, but he wasn't sure how long he could hang on. Rising to his knees without missing a stroke, he reached between their joined bodies, messaging her exposed clit.

Georgie screamed, her back arching completely off the bed as her body convulsed. Bright lights danced in front of her eyes as she fell completely apart.

"Fuck!" Beau growled.

As she came, her pussy gripped him in a velvet vice, milking his seed as he emptied himself into her womb. He had never come so hard in his life. Unable to move, his body slumped to the bed, taking Georgie with him. He didn't want to leave her warm cocoon, not yet, so he maneuvered them so she could lie on top without him withdrawing.

He had been far rougher than he intended. This was her first time; he had planned on taking it slow and easy. Instead, he had rutted like a dog in heat, not giving any thought to her virginal state. He felt like shit and more than just a little afraid he was going to frighten her off. He had to make it up to her somehow.

"Georgie?"

A soft little snore was his only reply. Georgie had fallen fast asleep.

Chapter Three

"Lord, what have I done?" Georgie watched Beau's car fade in a cloud of dust down the dirt road. She waited for the guilt and the regret to swamp her, she was almost wishing for it. There was none. The rational part of her knew she had probably just destroyed any thought of a decent marriage. She was no longer a virgin. How would she possibly explain that one? Still, she didn't feel even a twinge of shame. She felt like she'd been pleasured well and maybe even a little bit treasured. And no one knew yet. Her father, yes, but no one else had a clue where she had spent her night. "I have to get out of here." Staying couldn't be an option. She needed to get back to a world she understood. It was far too tempting to stay here and let Beau take care of her. What would that make her then?

Within ten minutes, she was dressed and trudging down the long, dirt road back to her father's house. Many hours later, she knew she had made a very painful mistake. By the time she finally made it to her father's house and club, she knew she had developed quite a few blisters. To make matters worse, she couldn't find her clothes, so she had to wear what she could find — a pair of Beau's old dungarees and one of his shirts. The pants were so big, she had to use one of his ties to keep them from falling off her hips. On her feet was a pair of his old work boots with no socks. By the time she trudged into the yard her feet were screaming in pain. She was sure her feet were damned near covered with blisters, and damned if they didn't hurt like a son-of-a-bitch.

Cursing her own foolishness in thinking she could walk the many miles between the Dupuis spread all the way to her father's house, she made her way around to the back of the house. How many miles she had walked she couldn't say. Although it had been midmorning when she left, it was fast approaching dusk. Customers would be arriving soon. She had no idea if she would be able to work much tonight, probably not, but she was going to give it a try. It would at least take her mind off of what she had just walked away from.

"Georgiana! What are you doing here?"

She was snapped out of her mental griping by the irritated voice of her father. She had been so intent on making it to the pump to get some relief for her aching feet she hadn't noticed him standing on the back porch. She had wondered what she would say to him about where she'd been all day and night, but then, sounded like he already knew. What was she doing here? This was her home!

Then she noticed the trunk hefted over her father's shoulders. Her trunk. Or Beau standing right behind him with two new looking suitcases. Or Beau's car that looked to be packed to the gills. Yeah, her father knew where she had been alright. And apparently, he was none too concerned.

"I thought I lived here, Daddy."

She had to fight to keep her voice level, but she couldn't keep the hurt, betrayed look at bay. How could he do this to her? She was his daughter! Yet, here he was, throwing her to the first rich white man that came along. She knew she was being grossly unfair. Beau was hardly the first rich white man that had offered money for a "little time" with his daughter. She knew that. Juke joints were notorious for attracting the idle rich who wanted to walk on the other side of the tracks for a while. But he had always managed to keep her away from all that. Why was he suddenly so willing to throw her to Beau now? Was she suddenly no better than a common whore to him?

Determined not to be kowtowed by the two men looking at her so intently, she started toward the pump as if they weren't moving all her belongs out of the only home she had ever known. She didn't want to think about bullheaded men who thought they knew what was best for her. They would not turn her into a kept woman, the one thing she had no desire to be.

Her father made his way down the porch stairs, put her trunk in Beau's car, then walked slowly back in the house. He didn't say a word. Georgie felt her throat clog with tears. Was he so interested in sending her away that he would not even say goodbye? Had she been that much of a burden?

She followed him, unwilling to just be kicked out of her home without an explanation, without a goodbye. Maybe he was upset she had left yesterday and not come back. She had left the laundry in the basket in the yard without a second thought. She did note the basket as well as the clothes that she had hung was no longer there. He had to know she had just walked off and left the things he had told her to do undone.

"Daddy?"

James Willard sat at the worn, scared oak table in the tiny kitchen, head in his hands. He tensed as she approached but didn't look up.

"Daddy, I'm...I didn't mean to..." Damn. What could she say? She had willingly gone off with a white man and stayed all night. There was no excuse for that. There was nothing she could say to make it better. "You can't even look at me?" Tears she had tried to swallow flowed freely down her cheeks as she tried to will her father to look up at her. She was a disgrace; yet, there was no shame in what she had done even now. Only pain knowing she had failed her father. And if she had to do it all over again, she would probably do the same exact thing. Oh she was going to hell on the express train. "I'm sorry."

At her broken, whispered apology, her father finally lifted his head. There were no tears, though his eyes were as red a man on a weeklong drunk.

"Ain't nothing to be sorry for, Georgie. You go n now. Ain't no place for you here."

She felt the breath freeze in her lungs. No place for her? In a juke joint? Because she had fallen just once, she had to leave? It wasn't as if her father was a paragon of virtue. Anguish warred with anger as she just stared at her father.

"No place for me? You would throw me away because I...Because I made one mistake?" He was still there, waiting silently at the door. She didn't have to look behind her to know he was there, she could feel his eyes on her. What was more, she could feel his anxiety. She couldn't be bothered with trying to sooth him now; in truth she shouldn't have cared. He had gotten what he wanted. Now apparently he was about to get a whole lot more. This was not what she wanted. She felt the cell door of her life closing in on her, and she wasn't sure she was strong enough to face it. "Daddy?"

Tired brown eyes rose and looked at her so sadly she wanted to sink through the floor. Why had she gone with Beau yesterday? She could have told him to stop, she could've said no. It was too late to go back now. She tried to swallow the tears, but they kept on flowing. Her father's heart was broken.

She could see it. And she knew she had done this, and there was nothing she could do to make it better.

"Don't you dare go on blaming yourself for this girl, you hear me?" James Willard's voice might have sounded harsh, but his face told a far different story. "Georgie, girl you ain't never had too many choices, not matter what you might've dreamed up in that head of yours. This is for the best. That boy can take care of you better than most." He sighed, shaking his head as if he had committed some great crime. Georgie wanted to scream for him to stop, that it was her fault. Nothing came out though as her father went on. "I had choices too, and maybe I should've made better ones. I threw your future away because I was selfish. Didn't want to dance to nobody else's music. I drug you down, Georgie. No decent man would've ever married you, and I couldn't've protected you after too much longer. Go. Be safe. Live your life for you, girl, and stop worrying about busy bodies and hypocrites. He'll take care of you. I wouldn't never let you leave if I didn't know for sure. Go on now, before people come nosing around."

Georgie couldn't move. Why was he saying these things to her? Why didn't her father want her anymore? Wasn't a father supposed to love his children no matter what they did? He hadn't been married to her mother, yet he had never looked at another woman as far as Georgie knew. So why would he punish her like this for one stupid, stupid mistake?

She was being pulled out of the place she had always known as home, unable to fight it.

"Georgie?"

Damn it all to hell! That voice! Lord, but would she ever stop being affected by that voice? All sweet and slow, even despite her anguish it set her heart racing. Already she felt herself getting all wet and needy.

"Baby, look at me."

That she could not do. Those fathomless baby blues could drown a woman. Her eyes darted everywhere about the dirt yard, everywhere but at him. He held her from behind like she was going to get away; he seemed fond of doing that, not stopping until her body was flush against his front. Where would she run? She had no place else to go. She wasn't even a little surprised by the bulge pressing against her back. God and the angels help her, but she wasn't able to break away. The smell of him, all masculine and delicious surrounded her, making her knees a little weak. She hurt so bad, but she melded into him seeking solace. The cause of her downfall, her great mistake, and she was helpless but to lean on him. He would try to take the pain away. That's just who Beau was.

Despite being hungry, thirsty, and tired beyond reason, her senses sprang to life as soon as his big body surrounded hers. The man inspired all kinds of needs deep in her belly that didn't have a dang thing to do with the fact she hadn't had a bite to eat all day. Even as her heart, bruised and battered, ached to crawl back home, she wanted to crawl into this man's arms, bury herself into his side and never look up. Did that make her wicked? A wanton of the worst sort? Who the hell was she?

"Come on, Georgie, honey. Talk to me."

Despite her resolve, despite knowing this way lead nowhere but heartbreak and a life of pain, she melted in his arms. Her eyes drifted shut, her head leaning over ever so slightly to give him access to her neck. Lord, but his lips felt so good there. Who else in the world could make something so wrong feel so right? She was going to burn alright, Beau being the fuel and the fire.

"Let me take you home, baby. Please?"

She was no fool. That was no question. She moaned as he lightly bit her ear, nibbling the lobe just a little. His arms tightened around her, his hands rubbing her stomach, her arms. He didn't touch her inappropriately, maybe because her father was so close by, maybe not to scare her away. Despite her continued silence, she knew, too, she was telling him yes. Tears she had been holding back by sheer force of will fell silently down her cheeks. A small nod was all he seemed to need. He swept her up in his arms to take her away.

This was not her home anymore. Whatever her father's reasons, he had made it clear he found Beau acceptable to take her away. Maybe because he knew Beau would never hurt her intentionally. James Willard had known Beau all the younger man's life. There was no point in being mad at him. He loved her, raised her the best he could all alone. Many women had tried to "reform him for the sake of his child," but from the very beginning, it had been the two of them against the world. He'd never mistreated her or allowed anyone else to do so.

Realistically, Georgie knew her father was between a rock and a hard place. She was not too blind she didn't see the looks from the less than savory characters that came here night after night. She heard the whispered comments about her body, about what they would like to do to that body. As much as she held out hope for an offer of marriage from a good, decent man, the ribald remarks around her had increased with each passing year. If a group of men decided not to wait for her or her father's permission…she shivered at the possibility.

Beau arranged her carefully on the passenger seat before closing the door and fairly running to get in himself. He didn't show it, but Georgie could tell he was angry. His body radiated with it, but he never raised his voice.

Whereas before she had been silent because she just felt like being ornery over drastic changes in her life she could do nothing about, now she was just a touch scared. Was he mad at her for leaving? She watched a telltale tick in his chiseled jaw as he drove. What would he do or say when they got back to the cozy house that would be as much a heaven as a hell? Her own agitation increased the closer they came to the Dupuis property. By the time they drove up to her new home she was almost in a panic.

Why hadn't he said anything else? Was all that sweet talking just a ruse to get her back here? What sense did that make?

"Go on in," Beau ordered softly. There was still not a trace of anger in his voice, but she knew it was there boiling right beneath the surface. "I'll be a minute or so."

Swallowing the acrid taste of panic, Georgie slid out of the car to make her way with agonizing care up to the door. The lights where on in the kitchen and she could see a shadow moving around inside. Ida. Maybe the older woman would have something for her poor feet.

Georgie hadn't made it more than a few steps before the car door slammed behind her. Beau, cursing up a storm, stalked right up to where she stood frozen in terror. Why, she wasn't quite sure. He wouldn't hit her; she knew that. But the look of fury on his face rooted her to the spot. Beau was devilishly playful, amicable, and easy going. This Beau was someone she had never seen before.

A little squeak eked out as he bent and seized her in his arms without missing a stride. He carried her into the house, through the kitchen right past a surprised Ida.

"Ida, would you please bring some Epsom salt in to the bathroom, please?" he threw over his shoulder and kept right on going.

He didn't stop until he set her carefully on the same bed they had shared last night. Georgie felt her face heat at the thought. How could she not think about it? Who knew conjugal relations would be so, so…well, feel so dog gone good? Better than good. She had felt like she was flying and crashing at the same time. When he kneeled on the floor at her feet, her face got even hotter. She couldn't help but remember when he had been in a similar position last night. Oh, sweet Mother Mary, that wicked tongue was capable of miracles!

"Damn it, Georgie!" Beau hissed as he eased the oversized boots off her feet. By the look on his face, it must have looked pretty bad. "Did you want to get away from me that bad?"

Her feet had hurt, but she had just thought it was because she'd walked more than a few miles to get home. Now she could see her feet were a bloody mess. Blisters had formed, some popped, and the flesh had been torn away in bits and pieces. She winced more from how bad they looked than from any real hurt. Maybe she was just too tired, or maybe it would come later.

It was the pain in his voice that tore her to pieces. It hadn't been Beau she was running from. Not really. She wanted to escape the way he made her feel. She wanted the future she couldn't have if she stayed with him, the future that was now her destiny. Beau she could love with every fiber of her being. It was being the other woman, the dirty little secret that would kill her. Having any children that might have been called "bastard" or "breed" would kill her. Loving Beau was the easy part.

She wanted to tell him, tried to find the words, but he was on his feet and into the bathroom before she could find the words. The wooden floors groaned with his movements, the pipes moaned as they came to life. It was as if they too could feel the pain radiating from him.

There was nothing she could do to alleviate it. She wanted what she could never have, she couldn't help that. There wasn't a damn thing either of them could do about it. Marriage between them was out of the question. Not only were there laws against it, they would be run out of town on a rail even if they could find a preacher who would do it anyway. No, what Georgie wanted, Beau couldn't buy her. He couldn't charm his way into getting it for her. No amount of his family's money or prestige could get it for her. Still, she could not help it. She didn't really just want to be a wife, she finally admitted to herself. She wanted to be his wife.

*****

Beau shut his eyes to try to banish the pain. No matter what he did, it ripped through him, slicing from heart to the gut. Damn it all to hell! Why couldn't she be born white, or he black? It was some kind of twisted Romeo and Juliet tale that would probably end just as badly.

No! Not that!

Neither he nor Georgie would die; he would never allow it. But he could not give her what he knew she wanted, no matter how badly he might want to.

Georgie was finally asleep, her abused feet all treated and bandaged. Ida had wanted to do it, but he could not stand the thought of anyone else's hands on her. He needed to care for her. It was his fault after all. He should have waited, just a little while more, he never should have brought her here. He should have found a way to whisk her off to Canada where they could be married.

He just couldn't leave now. Times were hard, and his family had a responsibility to the people of Blakeley. His father needed him to try to help dole out as much work as they could, equally and fairly between hard hit families. Too many people were leaving. His own best friend's father had shot himself when the market crashed. Manny Davis had not been able to face his wife and child after he lost everything. Beau's friend, Fulton, had gone west looking for work, wringing a promise out of Beau to look after his mother. In true southern fashion, Mrs. Davis refused to admit anything at all was amiss.

Things like these kept him here, but an irresistible draw pulled him to Georgie. He could no sooner leave her alone than he could stop breathing. He was a selfish bastard. He couldn't blame her if she hated him. But he couldn't give her up either. Selfish he may be, but she was like a drug to his soul, and he didn't want a cure.

Letting out a harsh breath, Beau turned to go back into the house. He needed to be near Georgie, to hold her even though she was finally sleeping. He needed to make sure she was in his bed — their bed. *Where she belonged.*

Despite the absolute conviction he had in the thought, he couldn't help but question the wisdom of making her his as he had. If there had been any other way...

Hell that was a lie. When her father had come to him telling him about the offers he was getting for his baby girl, Beau had seen red. Georgie was no whore.

You made her one, his mind whispered the condemnation.

He had wanted her for years, he admitted that. He'd watched from afar as the adorable little girl had grown into a coltish adolescent whose promise of beauty was far too evident to his liking. She had been so damned young when she had begun to develop curves that had driven him half out of his mind.

But he had waited. Watched closely as she matured. He hadn't wanted to ruin the fantasies of the future he knew she had harbored. Innocent dreams every girl had, white or black, of a strong man who loved her, a good decent marriage complete with children and a little house.

Funny how watching a woman so closely gave a man insight into things most men never bothered noticing. She drank in the sights of happy little families when she went to town. The look of longing on her face tore him up. Georgie wore her heart on her sleeve, making it too easy for others to hurt her. How he wanted to make those uptight bitches with their snide remarks pay. Georgie would have never been accepted into their closed-minded circles.

He had done what he could behind the scenes. He had been paying for her upkeep since she turned fifteen, giving her father money monthly to make sure she had any and everything she needed. Even when he had been sent off to school up north, he made sure James had money.

James Willard had been furious at first when Beau approached him. But James knew the truth. No decent man would be courting the illegitimate daughter of the juke joint owner. She had been considered damaged goods from her birth; not that she was, but folks in Early County were simple minded about some things. The phrase "sins of the father" was taken as the gospel. They both knew it. It would have been kinder for

Beau to offer to sponsor her to move away from here, but she would have never done it. If he were honest with himself, he would admit he couldn't have let her go. She had no family elsewhere. There would be no one to see to her safety. Her father would not leave, though why Beau didn't know.

He had researched a place for them; somewhere they could be together out in the open. Canada or the far west were their only options. He didn't want to chance the west, not with so many southerners headed that way looking for work. If things weren't so bad here, maybe they could have found peace out near the Pacific somewhere…but they were. Families were moving in droves, and they were taking their long-held prejudices and sense of morality with them.

Slipping into the bed, he pulled his woman into his arms. They would find a way soon. He would work it out. How long could the damn Depression last anyway? Until then, he just had to make this enough for the both of them. He could make her happy if she just gave him the chance.

Closing his eyes, he let the peace her presence brought him soak into his soul. They were meant to be. He knew it; surely, she knew it too. This was nothing like his father and Ida; Georgie wasn't his piece on the side, his private plaything, or his secret life. Georgie was his life. He just had to make her believe. He could do that. Lord, please let him be able to do that.

Chapter Four

Lily Anne Dupuis had lived with humiliation for years. Her husband had paraded his whore under her very nose, in her own house from the day she moved into the Dupuis mansion. While he might have tried to hide his tawdry liaison from her in the beginning, halfheartedly at best, he had stopped being inconspicuous a very long time ago. Every night, rain or shine, he walked boldly out the door and made the short trek to the much smaller house behind, not returning until morning.

Ida Monroe might have held the title of Head Housekeeper, but she was no one's maid. Lily snorted as she watched the woman in question through the parlor window. Sure, the voluptuous black woman planned and cooked all the meals, but as far as Lily was concerned that was about all she did. And, even that was merely another way the whore was catering to Lily's husband. That was, after all, her real occupation. She hated the statuesque black woman with every fiber of her being. She would kill her dead if she didn't live in fear that Branford would return the favor. Nothing, not even her fragile constitution, could keep her husband from his whore and her bastards.

Lily had planned her marriage to the prince of Early County—all of Southern Georgia really—very carefully. Her family had been in desperate need of money, and their only hope was for Lily Anne to marry well. She had been hell-bound not to simply bag a rich man; she wanted the richest, most handsome man in the area. Unfortunately, Branford had not been easy to drag to the altar. With the assistance of both parents, she had been forced to get him drunk during a weekend party at her parents' home in Bainbridge and crawl into his bed. It was a masterful plan, coming together like clockwork.

She had climbed on top of him more than once, trying desperately to get pregnant. It was not a must that she conceive, seeing as how her father was all set to bust in her door at first light. There would be a tiny scandal, but as soon as she was Mrs. Branford Dupuis all would be forgiven. Being with child was merely an insurance policy. And it had worked—all too well.

What Lily had not planned on was the skill of her husband as a lover. She could have loved him; she had wanted to love him. Despite tricking him into marriage, she had briefly hoped for a happy marriage. She had done what she had to do, but Branford didn't need to know that. Every second of that night was burned in her subconscious forever.

The memory of his kisses still burned her skin, the ghost of his hands from long ago sent shivers of excitement down her usually stiff spine. Even now, she felt her center moisten from the recollection of just one night. He had been so forceful, so masterful. Although she had lead in the beginning, Branford had turned the tables on her feeble attempts at seduction, all the while calling another woman's name.

Clutching the ornate chair in which she sat, Lily felt a familiar sense of rage wash over her, blurring her vision in a red haze. Branford had not touched her since that night. Oh, he had married her alright, taken her from the bosom of her family, paid off her father's debts, set her up as the reigning queen of society. But he had not touched her. He never spoke to her without cause. He had seen through the trap, had known immediately he had been set up, and he had never forgiven her. And, he had never allowed her to be a true mother to her own son.

Now her son had fallen into the same trap that ensnared her husband. Her perfect boy was bewitched by forbidden lust, and Branford approved. Hell, for all Lily knew, Branford had orchestrated this, influenced Beau, led him down this path. Her husband had encouraged Beau to install his whore on the same property in which his mother lived! It was an affront to her and society in general. The whispers she had to deal with during tea! Trying to find a decent woman to marry Beau was becoming almost impossible. No mother wanted to send her daughter into a household infested with not one, but two, black whores!

For years, Lily had borne her shame with dignity. She had kept her head held high and preserved. She had held out hope one day her husband would turn to her, if not as husband should turn to his wife, but at least as a friend. That was never going to happen. Well, she would not allow her only child to fall into the same trap.

Looking down at the letter in her hands, a rueful smile graced her thin lips. Normally, she would never even consider such a request. She would have burned it and sworn on a stack of Bibles she had never seen, much less read such a thing. Thank goodness, she had had the presence of mind to keep in touch with her husband's distant relatives in England. They were titled after all, an important notch in her social belt.

Beau was conscientious about world affairs. Much like his father, she knew he followed the goings on in Europe, devouring every news item they could. At least the boy still came by Sunday afternoons, if not for dinner, for a visit. They often argued about the crazy German man whose name constantly escaped her. Something horribly foreign sounding by her way of thinking. Beau thought the United States should intervene, Branford believed it was none of their business. Beau had graduated from West Point and had spent four years as an Army Air Corps pilot afterward. Yes, this little tidbit would be perfect to tear her son out of the arms of that sorceress.

Just three more days, and she would play her card. Beau had such a strong sense of right and wrong, excepting the abomination he was laying up with currently. There was no way he would say no. All she had to do was wait until he was gone, and then Lily could rid herself of at least one of her greatest sources of pain. Surely a little time away from temptation would cleanse her boy of his unnatural craving. She would not allow her son to become the rotten man her husband was. She would at least save her child.

*****

Fall was beautiful in South Georgia. Though some trees had turned gold, russet, burnished copper, they were surrounded by ones that were deep emerald year round. The grass was every bit a lush as it was in spring, completely blanketing the ground. Despite the fact so many had been devastated by lack of rain and crops all over not only Georgia, but also Alabama, Mississippi, reaching up into the Midwest, and were failing, here vegetation flourished.

Dust Bowl is what the papers and radio were calling it. Coupled with the Crash and the following Depression, there was a heavy, dark cloud that seemed to have engulfed the entire country. The Deep South had been hit especially hard. Many families were moving west, in anxious hope for greener pastures. Parents watched with vacant eyes as their children starved, men left their families in search of work never to return. Though there were some jobs programs, few reached this far south, and when they did, they were snatched up by the most aggressive, leaving late comers despondent.

Despite all that was going on around her, Georgie felt none of the pain and anguish of her fellow countrymen. She had told herself she would never be happy being Beau's woman but not his wife, and she had believed it at the time with her whole heart. But how could a body not feel sated, lying on top of the man who had opened up a world of possibilities?

The breeze whispered through the trees, cooling her bare skin that had so recently blazed with desire for the man beneath her. Her eyes closed, she listened with half an ear to the deep baritone reading poems in praise of her beauty. Shakespearian sonnets actually. Beau loved the classics, and he had opened up a whole new world to her, insisting they read together once a day.

Georgie had never gone to school, but her father had made sure she knew how to read, write, and cipher figures. The only two books she had ever read prior to moving in with Beau were the *Bible* and *Uncle Tom's Cabin*. Now she read *Romeo & Juliet*, *Beowulf*, *The Canterbury Tales*, and many, many more. She didn't care for the epic adventures Beau favored, like *Moby Dick* or *Gulliver's Travels*, but she adored tragedies and romances. Her secret delight was the naughty books Beau sometimes broke down after sundown with a wicked gleam in his eyes. *One Thousand and One Arabian Nights* never failed to thrill her, but the illegal printings of ancient pillow books from India made her both blush and wet whenever they appeared suddenly after supper.

"You keep wiggling like that and you're gonna find yourself flat on your back," Beau growled playfully, running a single finger down to the base of her spine.

How was a body supposed to keep still with him touching her like that? Just to be ornery, she moved her hips directly against his heavy, steadily growing rod. It was impossible not to feel just a little bit powerful by the way his heartbeats sped under her cheek and way he could not help but move his large hand to cup one butt cheek, grinding against her. She knew this could not lead where she wanted — with Beau buried deep inside her. He had promised his mother he would come to Sunday supper today. They had probably been out here far too long already.

With a deep sigh, she lifted her upper body to look down at her man. Desire warred with duty, making his jaws clench and eyes screw tightly shut.

"Shouldn't we be leaving soon?" Although there was laughter in her voice, she didn't really want to go.

Still, his mother was his mother. Georgie would have given her right arm to have had a mother as well as a father growing up. She would never do anything to keep him from visiting his own mother. The woman probably hated her with a passion, but that didn't make her any less her lover's parent.

"We can steal a few minutes," was the husky reply.

Her breath caught when he opened his eyes to stare up at her. Yearning had turned the blue orbs almost black. He stared at her with such intensity she shivered. Instead of one hand on her backside there were now two, the book of sonnets lay abandoned in the grass.

"Give me your lips."

Georgie didn't even think about denying him, he was riding the edge already. Usually she would have delighted in teasing him until he pinned her underneath his big body, plowing into her like a mad man. Not this time. When he lifted her, positioning her right above his waiting member, she didn't try to twist away. She needed this every bit as much as he did. Bracing her knees on the blanket on which they lie, she wasted no time sinking him into her sex.

Her gasp blended in time with his moan as she helped him slide home. Although they had just made love a few minutes prior, he still stretched her insides to their limit, filling her completely. Such a delicious fulfillment, she grudgingly let go of his succulent lips so she could sit up completely, placing her hands against his chest for leverage.

Three short months ago, Georgie had been horrified by the suggestion of this position. Beau had completely cured her of any, and all, trepidation when it came to all things sexual. He had taught her how to enjoy this and many other positions, many other methods of pleasuring one another. Being on top was one of her favorites because it allowed her to control her own pleasure.

Once seated completely, she began to slither her body forward then back again, not really lifting up and down, but rather stroking his cock against her inner walls. Her clit rubbed against his pelvis with every move, giving her clit as much attention as her overflowing pussy.

"Damn, baby you feel so good." Beau grasped both cheeks of her behind, grinding upward while pulling her down. "I could stay inside you forever."

She wished he could too. She would have told him so, but his thrusts were hitting her in a place that never failed to leave her breathless. Her belly clinched, trying to suck him in even deeper. The friction was killing her. It may have been her intent to torment her lover, but the feel of his thick, hard, length deep inside, the bundle of nerves in her little nubbin pressed against his steely, heated skin was beginning to make her frantic.

She couldn't take anymore of her own teasing. Sitting straight up, she moved her hips with more purpose, rising and falling with Beau's strong hands guiding the way.

"That's it baby girl, ride me. Shit, Georgie you look so damn good on top of me. My little pussy is tight around me. So wet."

His dirty talk should have horrified her, shocked her, but it sent an extra thrill racing all throughout her body. She lost her rhythm, unable to control the small tremors beginning from deep in her womb radiating outward.

"Beau, I can't," she cried out desperately, rocking her hips with wild abandon. She was so close, so damn close.

"Let me help you, sugar." In no time at all he had switched their positions, towering over her as he surged inside. "How's that, baby? Is that better?"

Oh, Lord yes! He filled her to the brink, stroking the inner fire to burn hotter, brighter. Birds flew from the trees in flocks at the chorus of cries emanating from the two of them. The slap of flesh against flesh probably scared off small animals so common in the surrounding woods. Georgie felt a familiar tightening in her lower belly. Her cries turned into pants as the tension building inside grew and grew, closer and closer.

Beau's hands gripped her hips in a bruising hold, assisting her frenzied quest. His own hips powered into hers on every down thrust, grinding her clit against his pelvis before starting the tormenting bliss all over again. She loved when he did that, making her feel him so deep inside her cervix, causing mini-spasms deep inside.

"Just like that," she whispered harshly. "Oh, yes, Beau, just like that!"

"Let go, Georgie baby. Come all over me. Let me feel you come."

That was all she needed to push her over the edge. Her world exploded in a cacophony of colors and sharp sounds. No matter how many times Beau took her there, it always felt like the first time. It always felt new and thrilling, like being on top of the highest mountain after an invigorating climb. Only better. Much, much better. Better than ice cream and chocolate combined.

"I love you so much, Georgie," Beau groaned as he came down from the incredible high they had reached together.

"I love you too, Beau. With my whole heart."

*****

Georgie had never told him she loved him before. Although Beau had declared his love until he was damn near hoarse, she had never returned the sentiment. When she had said it, all he had been able to do was hold her, crushing her against him as he tried to hold back tears that had gathered in his eyes at the simple words.

Those words had hardened his resolve, it had to speak to his father tonight. Even if he left Georgia with nothing, he was taking his woman to Canada, and he was marrying her.

Georgie deserved nothing less. Beau would move heaven and earth to give her what she desired most in this world, and that was respectability. She might be content to just live with him for a time, but sooner or later, she would begin to regret her choice. Not that it had been much of a choice.

Stopping his car in front of what had been his home three short months ago, Beau paused for a moment before getting out to face what was sure to be a painfully stilted supper with his parents. The two of them rarely talked. Although thus far, his mother hadn't mentioned his new living arrangements, it was obvious by her constant entreaties he settle down and marry.

There was no way in hell he would marry another woman. He couldn't even stomach the thought of anyone but Georgie beside him in bed at night. She was the first thing he ever wanted to see in the morning. His entire world had narrowed and focused on one thing—making Georgie happy. The rest of world be damned.

With a sigh of resignation, he climbed out of his car and headed on inside. As usual, the house felt cold, much more like a mausoleum than a family home. Both his parents were seated in the front parlor, far away from one another. Branford was nursing a bourbon in a chair close to the empty fireplace while Lily stitched a sampler by the French windows.

His mother jumped up, rushing to him as soon as he walked through the parlor door.

"Beau! Well, I cannot imagine what has kept you away from home for so long!"

He knew without a doubt she knew very well what kept him from home. But Lily was ever the Southern Belle. She would not admit her son had a colored lover for all the money in the world. She would blithely ignore Georgie's existence even if Beau marched her naked through this very house.

Beau bent down for the perfunctory kiss on the cheek that was little more than a barely there brush of the lips against his skin. The hands that clung to his arms were as cold as they were boney, the chill seeping through the fabric of his shirt. She was surprisingly strong despite her frail, petite appearance. He sometimes wondered if she was a secret pugilist when no one was around.

After properly greeting his mother, he moved into the room to greet his father. Without a thought, the older man reached into his jacket pocket to hand him a handkerchief to wipe his mother's lipstick off his cheek. Only then did Branford shake his son's hands, asking the required questions. "How was he doing? Was everything alright out at the house?" Because Beau was in charge with the day-to-day running of the peach orchards and various vegetable crops, he rarely saw his father nowadays. Branford had an office in town from which he overlooked his various statewide properties, three of which were rented out by the federal government, shipping enterprises, import and export businesses, as well as the various foreign investments spread out on four of the seven continents.

Despite the normalcy of the questions, Beau could not help but notice the questions in his father's eyes. Beau allowed him to see just a glimpse of his happiness. Maybe it would make the talk they needed to have later a little easier. He doubted it, but Beau hoped against hope Branford would understand, not that it mattered. He was leaving. It was the only thing he could do.

Supper was every bit as painful as Beau had expected. Having been gone for a while, he was able to observe the two people who had given him life with new objective eyes. He noticed how his mother tensed every time Ida came into the dining room to place something on the table, or to clear away plates. He noticed the way his father's eyes followed the other woman even while his wife silently seethed. Branford's face was carefully blank, but Beau didn't need to see emotion to know what his father was thinking.

Turning his attention back to his mother, he noticed the tiny frown lines on Lily's once serene face. He had always wondered if she knew about Ida, now he knew. Then again, how could she not know? Although Ida's husband was very light, her children were all clearly of mixed race.

How humiliating it must be for both women. One suffering her husband's infidelity right in front of her face, the other forever branded a fallen woman, nothing more than master's bed slave. Didn't matter slavery had been outlawed for over seventy years, that was what she was.

This was the life he and Georgie had to look forward to if he didn't act now. It was not a pretty sight. Bitter tension filled the very air of the large room as each person studiously tried to ignore the elephant in the room. The only sound for a while was the tinkling of silver against china.

Clearing his throat, Beau tried to fill the terrible silence.

"Daddy, I need to speak with you after supper if you have the time."

Calm, respectfully, without giving a hint as to the subject. Beau was proud of himself.

"There hasn't been trouble out in the fields has there?" Branford inquired, all ears.

"No, sir," he hurriedly answered to disabuse his father of any such notion.

In fact, crops where surprising plentiful. The drought was hitting many pretty hard, yet the underground springs they ran under their crops had yet to dry out. He had no idea how long their luck would last, but as for now, he was grateful.

"There is something else I would like to discuss with you. Something personal."

Branford gave a sharp nod, but didn't press further. Beau knew his father had gathered that whatever it was, it was about Georgie. All he could do was to pray to God his father would not make him choose, because his choice was already made.

"Oh, no!" Lily exclaimed clasping her napkin to her chest. "Tell me they didn't write you too!"

His mother looked horrified, a single tear sliding out of the corner of one eye. She was good, but Beau was in no way fooled. There might be a tear in her eye, but she was passively gleeful about something.

"What are you blathering about Lily Anne? The boy needs to talk to his father, nothing wrong with that. And here you go with all your dramatics!" Branford sighed, already dismissing his wife as his attention returned to his food.

"Why, your cousins in England, Lord and Lady Howard. Something about needing pilots and the German man, the one y'all hate so much," Lily sniffed into her napkin. "England is requesting volunteers for the Royal Air Force against the bombers from Germany. Well, you can read it for yourself right here."

Although she threw the letter that seemed to appear out of nowhere at Beau, it was Branford who snatched it up with a smoldering glare in his wife's direction.

He couldn't prove it, but Beau swore he saw a grin on his mother's face before she began wailing loudly, running from the room.

"Damn devious bitch planned this!"

That his father had actually directed the profanity at Lily shouldn't have shocked Beau, but it did. He knew his parents could barely tolerate each other, he had no idea his father harbored such deep animosity.

"You are not going!" Branford thundered, balling the letter in his fist and throwing it across the room. "I don't give a damn how much you think you have to go, I forbid you from going! Take your little gal and run to Canada. It's what you want to do anyway. I will arrange it. But you will not be going to England to fight their damn war!"

With that final word, Branford stormed from the dining room, heading toward the kitchen. Beau sat frozen in his seat, distantly hearing Ida's soft exclamation and then the back door slamming shut. He sat even when the girl Ida used to help her in the kitchen scurried in to clean the food platters and dirty dishes off the table and scurried back into the kitchen.

He had no idea how long he sat there, but it was full dark before he moved with leaden feet to collect the letter his father had thrown to the floor earlier. Turning on the light, he scanned to contents, his heart dropping to the pit of his stomach. He had warned his father Hitler would not be happy until he controlled all of Europe, and beyond. Sooner or later, they would be drawn into this war. In the meantime, people were dying as a consequence of the U.S.'s policy of non-interference.

He had to go. His honor demanded it. Later he would wonder how Branford had known about his plan to take Georgie to Canada. For now his only thought was how was he going to explain it to her?

Chapter Five

No matter how hard she tried to act like she didn't care, Georgie couldn't seem to keep her eyes dry as she watched Beau pack his trunk. Anything could happen while he was over there, who knew if she would ever see him again. There was no way she could stay here, despite the fact that was what Beau wanted her to do.

"Promise me you won't leave," Beau said suddenly as if reading her thoughts. "You will have everything you need right here. Now that you know how to drive the car, you can visit your father *during the day*."

She bristled a little at the implication. She grew up in her father's house. She was not too good for it now. Besides that, how the hell could he expect her to live out here all alone? She would die of boredom. That is, if some vagrant didn't get her first. Their little love nest wasn't even in view of the big house. No one would hear her scream until it was too late.

Ignoring his plea, she walked over to straighten his collar, which didn't need straightening at all. "Take care of yourself over there, you hear. Maybe I will be here when you get back."

He wasn't about to let it go, but then she knew he wouldn't. "We can still get you a place in town if you like. Or you could move in with Ida, she would be glad to have you and…"

"No and no!" She raised up on her toes to kiss him in a effort to stop what she knew was coming. Didn't work.

He allowed her kiss for a moment before gently cradling her chin. "Georgie, please tell me you won't go back to your father's. It's not safe, not after…Not since you have been living here. With me."

Anger spread through her quicker than wildfire. "I lived there all my life and nothing has ever happened to me! You think just because I've been laying up with you all of a sudden someone is gonna jump me or something?"

"Yes, baby, I do."

His words were so quiet, she wanted to pretend she didn't hear them. But she did. Her anger melted as if it had never been, replaced by bone deep hurt that would not allow her to stop the tears that had been so close to the surface for the last month.

"How could you say that? I am not a whore!"

She tried to squirm out of the false shelter of his arms when he embraced her to hold her close, but Beau was not letting go.

"Baby, I know you're not. I'm sorry, Georgie. I am damned sorry, but you know it's true. If anything happened to you…"

Then don't go! The words screamed inside her head, but she couldn't bring them to pass her lips. So many times, she wanted to yell it, to cry it, to beg, but she wouldn't do that. She had known at the beginning this wouldn't last. She just hadn't counted on falling so hard, so fast.

Georgie felt as if her world was being ripped apart, and there wasn't a thing she could do to stop it. Of course, she would move back to her father's. She could not stand being here without Beau. This was their place, it would always be their special place, but she had to move on.

"Love me, Beau," she whispered to distract them both. It was the one thing she knew he couldn't refuse. "Just one more time."

His train left in a little over an hour, but she knew that wouldn't stop him.

She had expected a quick, wild coupling. That was what she thought she needed. Just one more time, so she would cherish memories forever. Instead, Beau made love to her slowly, worshipping ever part of her body. He held her so close, moving his hips languidly as if they had all the time in the world.

How could she not cry while being cherished, perhaps for the last time by the man who held her heart in the palm of his hands? Though tears ran freely down her face, he kissed them away, never stopping the bewitching movement of his pelvis. She couldn't count the number of times he made her come or the number of times he whispered "I love you" in her ear. All she knew was that when Beau left, he would take a piece of her with him, just as she carried a piece of him in her womb.

*****

"Take care of her for me, Daddy."

He was a man, therefore, he would not cry. But damned if he didn't want to cry right now. He watched the little white-washed house disappear from view and felt his throat clog, his eyes burning with unshed tears. If he could have, he would have packed her in his trunk and taken her with him. But this was something he had to do. He was able bodied, he knew how to fly bombers, and the man in power in Germany was more than just a menace. Beau knew in his gut this madness had to be stopped before it made its way here.

There were already Nazi propaganda organizations in German immigrant communities and some neighborhoods in the northeast, not to mention German sentiments finding their way into college and university campuses. Whether the powers that be knew it or not, they would be at war sooner or later. He had to go, if he could help in any way, he had to do this.

"I promise you, son, I will make sure no harm comes to your woman, son. You just make sure you take care of yourself and bring yourself back home to her. Then y'all can go to Canada, or Mexico, or wherever you intend to go."

Beau nodded and swallowed back his growing sorrow. It had been easier than he had thought to convince his father of why he had to do this. Unlike the scene in his dining room, Branford hadn't argued much, he hadn't yelled, or threatened. He had just nodded his head tiredly and helped Beau make arrangements to ensure Georgie would be alright until he came back. And he would be coming back. Not even death would keep him from his woman.

*****

Branford stood stoically as the train pulled out of the station. Beau was on his way to New York City, where he would fly to England. It was safer than taking a streamliner, with German U-boats manning parts unknown all across the Atlantic. As much as he wanted to blame his wife for this, he knew this was not of her doing. She had only expedited what had been inevitable. Let her believe she had won some kind of victory by tearing Beau and Georgie apart. The one thing that woman had never understood was love.

It had been obvious, at least to him, Beau was going to be with Georgiana at all costs, and woe to the fool who tried to keep him from her. Branford was no such fool. He understood all too well what it was like to love a woman to your very soul and never being able to claim her. Whereas Branford had been a pompous fool, allowing himself to be trapped into a loveless marriage to a spoiled vengeful woman, Beau had been very careful. The boy was like a dog with a bone. Nothing, no one, would ever stand in his way.

How he wished he had half the gumption his son had. He should have run away with Ida long ago. Instead he let his father influence him, he let his love and respect for his mother confine him, and worst of all, he had fallen for a poorly laid trap by a greedy grasping family.

Though Lily's parents had long since passed on, Branford found himself still supporting her ne'er-do-well brother and his family. He would never condemn his son to this kind of life, marrying the proper woman and living in civil hatred while the love of his life was not considered fit to do anything more than scrub his floors.

At least that was something he could do for his Ida. She had never scrubbed a floor, washed a dish, or laundered his clothes. She cooked, but that was only because she desired it. After condemning her to the life she now had, he had made it a point to hire enough household staff to where she would have to do nothing but supervise. In a real way, Ida was his wife, taking on all the wifely duties Lily had considered beneath her without the benefits of the title.

He had even had his half-brother, the product of his father and a former Dupuis plantation slave that had died in childbirth, marry her to give her the thinnest veneer of respectability. Because many slaves freed after the war took on the last names of their former masters, his children born to him by Ida carried his name. Three of them lived happy, productive lives in Canada, and one was trapped in war-torn France.

Branford rubbed his chest as the pain he had held back for so long cut through him. The tears he had held back for so many years flowed freely as he drove back to the plantation. So many mistakes, so many things he wished he could take back. It was far too late to take it back, he wasn't even sure he would if he could. He had long since stopped detesting his wife. He felt sorry for her mostly. She demanded what he could not give, and for that, he pitied her. It was every bit as much his fault as it was hers. Most of all, he would not give up Beau for anything in the world. A father was not supposed to have favorites, but Beau was so much his son. He was like a younger version of himself, only with a hell of a lot more common sense and a much stronger sense of right and wrong.

He was not close to his other children. Social mores had made that impossible. Of course, he could have thumbed his nose at society in general. He was the richest man in South Georgia; he could have done it and gotten away with it. But he hadn't done that. He hadn't wanted to disgrace Lily anymore than he already had. He heard the whispers, and he knew the rumors. No one dared to say anything to his face. Most of the town either worked for him or depended on his business. That had been a mistake. He more than anyone understood it was far too late to remedy that now.

Instead of taking the highway that led to the big house, Branford found himself headed toward the house Beau shared with Georgie. Despite what his son might have thought about him, Branford had eyes. Not only had he noticed his son's feeling for the young woman long ago, he had noticed the woman herself. Not in any kind of sexual way. Ida was more than enough woman for him.

He would have had to have been blind not to see the way the town folk treated the motherless girl. Branford made his business to know all that was going on in Early County. He knew how badly Georgie was treated for no other reason than he father failed to marry her mother before her birth. It was not so rare that a girl went to stand in front of the preacher with her belly full; hell, more than half the marriages in the county started that way. What had been unpardonable was that Martha, Georgie's mother, hadn't wanted to marry. She was the epitome of what the good folks called a "loose woman." As a result, Georgie was painted with the same brush.

No one had to tell Branford the girl was a virgin until Beau got to her. She was a good girl by all accounts. It wasn't fair the way the self-righteous townspeople of Blakely treated her, but now it would seem as if they had been justified in their belief Georgie was a nothing more than mattress trash.

With a heavy sigh that gave voice to the frustrated burden he knew he would have to make right. There was so such thing as going back in time and righting past sins, but he could make sure his son never walked down that crooked road. He would keep Beau's woman safe and secure, no matter the odds. And he would make damn sure his son did the right thing if…no, when he came back.

He had to come back. Beau was the chance to make all of Branford's sins right. It would not absolve him from the many mistakes and not-so-hidden sins, but Beau would be happy, and his woman would be happy. In the end, that was all a body could ask for out of this life. All the money and power in the world had not made Branford happy. He only really knew one of his five children. Beau would know every one of his, and they would all call him "Daddy" to his face.

"Did you forget something?" Worried suspicion was etched deep in Georgie's frown as she walked out on the porch as soon as Branford got out of the car. There was a broom clasped by her side.

Branford didn't believe for a second she had been sweeping. He had to admire her pluck. He had no doubt if he made one false move, she would have brained him but good. She was every bit the woman he had thought her to be.

"Did you tell him?" Branford looked pointedly at her stomach. Georgie was no fool, but then, neither was he. She had to have been at least three months along. He was frankly amazed his son hadn't realized Georgie was carrying, but he did.

"No." Georgie lifted her chin and stared at the man that was not only Beau's father, but the most powerful man in the county. She would not apologize for her action, nor would she be intimidated. No one was going to take away her child — in any way. If Branford even thought about suggesting she go see the root woman, she would be so far away from Blakely before he woke up from her braining him, no one would ever find her.

She was more than a little shocked when Branford simply sighed with a sad little smile and sank down to sit on the bottom step. He was rubbing his head with handkerchief though the oncoming dusk brought a cool breeze that belied the need to wipe sweat from his brow.

"May I ask you why?" was his only question.

She considered lying, but what would be the point now? Beau was gone, maybe never to come back. "He wouldn't have left, and he couldn't have lived with that."

Despite the fact that she felt Beau was ten times a fool for risking his life for somebody else's country, she understood Beau. It was the principle that mattered to Beau. He really felt this man, this Hitler and all his allies had to be stopped. She had learned so much more than fine literature from her lover. Beau shared everything with her, just like she was his wife.

But you're not his wife, she reminded herself harshly. *And you never will be.*

Swallowing the lump that had formed in her throat, Georgie perched on the rocking chair on the porch and considered Beau's father. He looked much older than she had ever noticed before. He was still rubbing his forehead, looking off in the distance at nothing in particular. Why was he here? What could he do about the baby?

"I would be much obliged if you would stay here at the house while Beau is…away," Branford finally asked her in a quiet, but gruff, voice. "We can't have anything happening to you or Beau's…my grandchild. Ida will be out to keep you company no doubt. I will be hiring some men here bouts to see to you, ah, security. I would really appreciate it if you only went to visit your pa during daylight. You need to go in town, you come see me. I will escort you every time you go." Standing to go, he finally faced the woman his son loved. "I'm not trying to boss you none. I just want you and the baby to be safe. I need to do this for my son. I will talk to your pa about all this, though I am pretty sure he will agree."

Branford walked with heavy steps towards his big fancy car, turning around as he reached the driver's side door. "Please try to stay away from the big house, especially when you start showing. Lily is…well, she ain't always right in the head, you ken? It might…It would just be best if she didn't see you."

Climbing into his car, Branford left a visibly stunned Georgie to stare after him in wonder. He had done what he could do about warning her, now he needed to make sure she was protected. No one on earth could help him out with that more than James Willard.

Chapter Six

He thought he could shake him, but the German was just too good. No matter how Beau maneuvered his small plane, the German plane was right on his tail. The first shots had just grazed his left wing, but he knew he was in serious trouble. His only prayer was to lead the German plane back to where Beau knew there were other full loaded RAF planes to get him off his ass. Bullets whizzed by so closely he could hear them. Damn it! He had to make it. The single-engine Lysander was for search and rescue, it was great for short take offs and landings, but it didn't give him much in the way of tricks once he was spotted.

He never should have volunteered for this mission over France. They needed someone to look for Resistance fighters, and flying was a hell of a lot better than sitting. He was much better in a Mosquito, which moved light as air, probably because it was made of wood. The most important thing was that it could outrun a German bomber.

More bullets made contact with the small plane and Beau knew he was going down. He had to make it to the tree line. Grayish black smoke billowed in the air around him, making it damn near impossible to see. Although he had on goggles, his eyes teared up from the smoke and fumes. If he could make it to the trees, he would be able to get away. He might be banged up a bit, but he would be alive. Diving toward the heavily forested area, he had almost made it when he lost control of the plane.

A large tree rose up in front of him, but there was no room to move around it. For a split second, all he could see was not the tree coming unstoppably closer and closer, it was Georgie.

*****

Marie saw the British plane as it fell from the sky, the demon red German plane on its heel. As soon as the British plane disappeared into the densely wooded forest, the German bomber pulled up and flew away. Knowing it would only be a matter of time before whatever German troops that were in the area got there, Marie ran as if the hounds of hell were after her to check on the pilot. If he was alive, she had to get him out of here fast.

"Gilles! David! *Venez vite!*"

The two bulky resistance fighters appeared as if from nowhere, having melted into the darkened scenery when the planes became visible. They had been waiting for a plane from England to take David safely out of the country. His sister had managed to steal intel with the troop movements from the local commander of the German forces and England was desperate for that information. David was a wanted man, he could not stay in France. They had negotiated to get him out and far away from the Germans. So far, no one was aware Marie was his sister. Gilles was the only living person with that knowledge, and he was born mute. Marie and David had managed to make it from Paris to Le Havre without detection, but their days were numbered. They were Jews, and in this war, Jews disappeared never to be heard from again. That was what had happened to the rest of their family. Marie was determined it would not happen to her youngest brother.

Thankfully, the aircraft had caught fire from the rear, and had not yet reached the cock pit. A quick feel to the pulse told Marie the man was alive, but definitely unconscious.

"*Nous devons le faire sortir d'ici!*" They had to get him far away from the crash site. Since there will be no escape for David tonight, they had to take him back to their headquarters.

Gilles and David didn't question her orders. Lifting what they assumed was a Brit pilot effortlessly, Gilles, who was a bear of a man, slung the unconscious man over his massive shoulders. They made their way through the forest, avoiding the roads where enemy troops were sure to be traveling. They had to stop and hide at least twice, but thankfully, the Brit did not gain consciousness. It took an hour, but they made it to the underground bunker on a formerly abandoned estate outside of Le Havre. It was now a German outpost, the last place they would look for a Resistance base.

The bunker was perfect; the access point was located far from the main house, connected by a concrete passageway.

There was electricity and running water, and it was reinforced so no sounds escaped the cramped space. It was cold and wet, but for now it was home. Marie ran a ragtag bunch of about twenty Resistance fighters, but only the three of them, Gilles, David, and Marie, knew where the base of their operations was located. From there they could contact the British without being detected by piggybacking off German communications lines.

Once the Brit had been laid on one of the cots, Marie set about cleaning and binding his wounds. She was spellbound by the beauty of the stranger's face, like an angel that had fallen into her lap, he was quiet simply beautiful. His lashes were long and lush, jet black against the paleness of his skin. His equally dark hair had been shorn short on the sides and back, but she could see hints of loose curls on top. Her eyes drifted down to a well-built body, now prone and immobile. She could not help but wonder what he would look like out of the drab uniform he wore. The only thing that stopped her was presence of Gilles and David, who hovered over her like mother hens.

There was no ring on his finger, but how could a man so blessed by the Fates look this good and not be taken?

A small smile played at Marie's lips. Taken or not, he was not married, and that meant he was fair game. This man was a long way from home. Though only the Channel separated him from his native land, it might as well have been an ocean. If they could get coordinates out any time soon, it would be a while before anyone came to rescue him. German activity was just too heavy. They had been warned if they did not meet the plane sent for David, it might be quite a while before another could be sent. There was plenty of time to get to know the Brit much, much better. War made strange bedfellows—literally.

*****

Lily saw the letter fall from her nerveless hand in a daze. The white paper was lazy in making its way to the gleaming wood floor, floating on the slight breeze as if it were something of beauty instead of an abomination. The thick paper was obscene in its stark, perfectly typed black lettering, the pristine smudge-free surface mocking her. The words were carefully chosen and composed as if they could offer her some small hope. If she knew how to cry, tears would surely have been falling down her cheek. Instead, all she could do was sit motionless as the words sank into her brain.

We regret to inform you... Valiant son shot down... Body not found...

It seemed so unreal, so inconceivable. Her son, her own son was lost. Perhaps forever. Shouldn't she feel something? Something other than this numbness, void of everything? There was no pain, no anguish, no...nothing. Just a cold emptiness that would never be filled again.

And she still couldn't cry.

It was all *her* fault, Lily decided with certainty. That colored woman had brought nothing but mischief. Well, something simply must be done about her. There was no reason for her to live on Dupuis land now. No reason for the little slut to even be alive. If her son was never coming home, then why should Georgina Willard even be allowed to breathe?

*****

"You have to go child, this ain't no game!" James rarely raised his voice to Georgie. He had never really needed to. Georgie had never been a disobedient child. He could not understand why she was being so obstinate now.

Never in his wildest dreams had James ever thought by encouraging his daughter to give up the false dream of marriage he would be putting her life in danger. If anything, he thought the opposite. The men who had been asking after her were not the kind any man would want his child associating with. No matter what Georgie believed, she would have never received an offer for marriage from any man worth his salt. She would have ended up in a dirt shack or far, far worse.

Beau Dupuis had been a godsend. James wasn't blind. He saw the beauty his daughter was becoming. When the young Dupuis had first come to him, asking him for his daughter, his first response had to been to shoot him where he stood. No matter what Georgie believed, the decision to allow Beau to pay for his child's care, the decision to agree to ever handing his baby over to a rich white man for anything less than marriage had plagued him. More than once he had contemplated picking up and leaving Georgia far behind.

But what would be different anywhere he went? He ran a juke, and that was all he knew how to do. It was far more money than share cropping, which often led to an early grave and a pile of debt for those left behind. What would Georgie do then, with no one to protect her?

Then there was Beau himself. That was one boy who just didn't give up. James' first "Hell no!" had been met with grace and acceptance, even understanding. The boy could have threatened him. He could have sent the sheriff or his father after him. Instead, he had nodded sagely.

"I understand, sir," Beau had told him. "I don't blame you for your reaction. Just know I will be back, and I will keep asking. I will do whatever it takes to get you to agree."

He had looked to where a very young Georgie had been coming in and out of the club, working to get the place ready for the night. Back then, she hadn't been allowed inside the club after the first customers arrived. Beau sighed, as her eyes never once turned his way.

"I aim to prove to you I love her," he had declared softly. "I would never allow any harm to come to her. I will work every day to convince you of that."

And he had. The boy had come back at least three times a week, careful never to approach Georgie herself, but rather aiming his arguments directly at James. For a year, Beau kept up the pleading, never giving up but never trying to intimidate, bribe, or blackmail him. James knew as long as he stayed here in Blakely, this was the best offer Georgie was going to get. He could have moved, but he had thought it would be too risky. He grew up here, and this was all he knew. Moving somewhere else, somewhere he didn't know his way around or wasn't that well known could have been a heap of trouble neither he nor his daughter knew how to deal with.

If he had any inkling this would happen, he would have never said yes. He would have high tailed it out of here so fast…

How could anyone have known Miss Lily Anne would lose her mind?

Despite the urgency in her father's voice, Georgie clenched her jaw mutinously, her body tightening in ready rebellion. Her mind refused to take into account the wild fear in the depths of his brown orbs. Through the window, she could see Branford Dupuis pacing a trench in front of his car. Ida flurried around her, packing everything small enough to fit in the trunks Branford had brought over with her father. For a while, Georgie tried unpacking even as Ida, carefully placed all the clothing in the house, hers and Beau's, inside those trunks, but her awkward pregnant body made it hard to move, so she simply wasn't able to keep up with the much older woman.

They were all making this seem far too permanent for her liking. Had any of them suggested just a brief time away, maybe a couple weeks in Savannah, or Thomasville, or even Atlanta she might have gone along with it. Sure Lily (because she could never call that crazy woman Miss Lily) would get over her anger soon. She was surely only upset her son was missing. What mother wouldn't be? For some reason, Beau's mother was blaming her, placing the blame on somebody she could punish. It would blow over sooner or later.

But moving to New Orleans? She didn't know a soul in Louisiana, much less New Orleans! How could they ask her to just pack up and move to a place she knew nothing about, where she would have no one. Branford had told her Ida would stay with her, for her and the baby's sake, but Georgie didn't want Ida. She wanted Beau.

Her eyes began to burn, but she managed to hold back the tears. It would do no good anyway. These people were convinced, and there was nothing she could say to dissuade them. They didn't understand. She couldn't leave the house, the home, she and Beau had made. The place her baby had been conceived.

How will Beau find me?

Georgie didn't care what those damn foreign people said. Beau was alive! She felt it in her soul he was alive and he was coming home. He promised her he was coming home, and when he did they would move somewhere they could be together. She ignored his claim they would be married; just being together freely would be enough for her, in her heart, she was already married. They had spoken vows to each other before he left, and Georgie believed he meant every word of his declaration of undying love.

She had no idea when it had been exactly that she started believing in Beau's promises, but she had. She had gradually gone from skepticism, afraid to believe, to believing in the impossible. Beau made it easy to believe. Never once had he treated her as if she was just someone to warm his bed. He shared everything with her, talked to her as an equal, patiently explained to her things she didn't understand without talking down to her. They listened to the news casts on the radio together, he taught her the importance of knowing what was going on in the world and making up her own mind about issues instead of taking someone else's word for it. He enjoyed arguing over events or issues. He never made her feel like she was any less than he. They talked about the books he introduced to her. He valued her opinion, which was rare in their world.

In many ways, they were far closer than most married couples she had witnessed. They were friends as well as lovers, and Georgie had come to depend on both in the time they had together. She had never thought she would ever be loved the way Beau loved her. She had never seen any woman loved like this. This was their home, hers and Beau's. She wanted to have their child here, in the place filled with their love. She had thought what she wanted most in the world was a man's name, decency, and family. Well, she had family here with Beau, and if their love wasn't decent then she didn't want that kind of decency. Beau filled all the empty spaces inside her and made her whole. This house was a symbol of that. How could she just walk away?

Unless…

Her sluggish movements stilled as the ugly head of doubt reared its head. Were they trying to get rid of her for some reason? Was this some elaborate scheme by Branford to appease his wife?

Soothing her hand absently over her protruding belly to calm the baby that had become as agitated as she, Georgie quickly dismissed the thought. Branford was a lot of things, but ruled by his wife was not one of them. He had made sure she had everything she needed since Beau's departure. He even brought her father out to visit her himself. Although Beau had left plenty of money, Branford made sure there was always food in the house, and he brought her the Sears catalogue so she could order clothes to fit her expanding frame without having to go into town. Sure enough, clothes arrived weeks later, without her paying a dime. It was as irritating as it was endearing. No, this was no ruse. They all really felt she needed to leave, and leave quickly.

Looking out of the window once more, Georgie felt shame creep over her. Branford had been so supportive, so much more than any white man should have ever been to his son's colored mistress. There was a growing sadness surrounding him since they found out about Beau being shot down. There were deep grooves in his face, making him appear far older in such a short amount of time. He rarely smiled anymore, and when he did, it was such a sad, forlorn gesture it made her cry. He would not try to get rid of her; she was his last connection to his son.

A bone deep chill replaced the burning shame. That meant Lily wanted her dead. What kind of a monster wanted a pregnant woman to die, knowing an innocent child would die with her? The tears that had threatened began to flow in silent rivers down her cheeks. What had she ever done to Lily? She had never flaunted her relationship with Beau, had never even seen the woman since she had been living here. Georgie had been talked about, talked down to, ignored, mocked, but never in her life had anyone hated her so much they wanted her dead.

What kind of hatred ran that deep? How could she ever hope to fight against it?

Chapter Seven

Beau leaned heavily on the makeshift crutch as he made the slow painful trek back to the Resistance headquarters. Marie and her crew were nice and all, but he had to get back to his adopted base in England. He had to send word he was still alive to his parents…to Georgie. With a heavy groan, he sank down on the hard cot, resting the leg throbbing in pain after the harsh workout. There had been no sign of English planes, no sign of hope.

"You do too much too soon," Marie scolded, hurrying to his side to check the bandages on the bandaged leg.

It hadn't been broken, unlike his ribs, but it had been banged up pretty bad. Marie had nursed him like a pro, hovering and mothering. Beau was downright uncomfortable with her constant touches. Maybe she was just trying to help, which he appreciated greatly, but there was something more in her eyes and in her touch. He didn't want to lead her on, or to give her any hope there would be anything between them. There was only one woman for him, and Marie was definitely not her.

"It's fine," he groused. He didn't want her touching him again. Somehow it just felt wrong.

Marie stood near the cot, frowning. Maybe he had been too harsh, but seriously, he couldn't take any more. The woman all but threw herself at him; when they were alone in the bunker, which was often, she went around in various states of undress, she took sponge baths in front of him, she always leaned in too close, and she was forever rubbing herself against him. Never mind it was damned irksome, it also left him cold. He suspected it had something to do with the fact that he was American. Once she discovered that little fact, there seemed to be a suspicious gleam in her eyes whenever she looked at him.

Shivering, Beau leaned back against the cold dank wall and closed his eyes. Damn it all his body hurt! His bones ached unbearably, his muscled screaming in protest. He was so very tired, but he needed to find a way to get out of here! He needed to get word to Georgie…His Georgie.

"I am only worried about you. If there were any British planes in the area we would have heard them over the radio…"

Marie kept chattering, but her voice sounded farther and farther away as if coming through some sort of long tunnel. His eyelids refused to lift, his body felt like a lead weight. He couldn't get up; he couldn't push Marie's hands away from his brow when she rushed toward him. He just needed to sleep for a little while. Then he would tell her he belonged to another. He would tell her he could never be with another. Just as soon as he got some sleep…

"He has a fever?"

Marie looked over her shoulder to where he brother David hovered. David did not like her plans for the American that fell into their laps. It was obvious to all of them that either this man didn't fancy women in particular, or he didn't particularly want Marie. When they had first brought him here, he had gone through three days of intense fever, in which he called out for someone named Georgie constantly. No one had asked about this "Georgie," who could have been either a male or a female. His cock had swelled during that time, his hips thrusting frantically into his imaginary lover.

Marie had no doubt this Georgie person was a woman, and she was determined to take her place. If she could only get the American to see this other woman was not here for him, but she was. Added to the fact that she wanted him beyond reason, should she succeed in seducing the American, she could possibly get him to marry her and take her, her brother, and possibly even Gilles to America, far, far away from this hell that had become their life.

"Bring me water and a cloth," Marie demanded, ignoring her brother's question as well as his frown. She did not need his censure.

As soon as David did as she directed she decided to send him away. He was supposed to be monitoring the short wave radio, but she didn't want him around for what she had planned. Gilles would not be here for several hours yet. All she needed to do was to get David out of the way.

"I will need you to sneak into the village for medicine," Marie told him while pretending to otherwise ignore him while bathing Beau's brows.

She felt him hesitate before moving off to do what she had bid. Although she could hear him making his way to the tunnels and finally out of the bunker, Marie waited, continuously bathing her patient for a few minutes more. She wanted to be absolutely sure she would not be disturbed.

After several silent moments, Marie carefully disrobed the unconscious man, careful not jar him. As she expected, the mumbling started soon, his penis rising long and hard as soon as she stroked her hand over his hot flesh. His eyes stayed shut, but the lids squeezed together in a mixture of agony and bliss. Her hand moved slowly at first, so as not to startle him, sliding the loose skin up and down until his hips began to move in time with her hand. As the organ expanded and hardened even more, she leaned down, circling the crown with her tongue before engulfing the head into her mouth with gentle suction.

"Georgie!" Beau groaned in his delirium.

Oui, for today, I will be your Georgie.

Taking his rod as far into her mouth as she could, Marie serviced him with her mouth until he was thrashing and groaning.

"Ah, Georgie baby, I missed you. I love you so much, baby. I am so sorry I left."

Closing her eyes, she imagined it was her he was calling out to. What would it be like to have this man love her with such devotion? Even though his hands tightened in her hair, he was careful not to pull too hard or to force himself down her throat. Even in his fantasies he cared for this woman so much he was careful with how he handled her. Marie could not conceive of such fidelity. Men had needs, as he so obviously did, yet he would not take what was freely offered. Instead, he retreated to his dreams to be with the woman he loved.

It was almost enough to make her regret her actions. Almost.

With one last loving lick, Marie quickly stripped and climbed on top of him. He was so thick, it took a moment before she could get fully seated. Beau still had not come out of his fevered sleep by the time she was moving. Anchoring her knees against his thighs, she lifted and descended slowly, savoring every ridge, every vein in his heavy tool. It had been so long since she had ever felt anything so divine, perhaps she never had. He filled her to the point of pain, but a good pain. Despite her best efforts to keep it slow and to delight in every stolen second, she moved faster, slamming him deeper and deeper inside. She had to bite her bottom lip until it bled to keep from crying out at the intense sensations vibrating inside her.

Beneath her, Beau thrust upwards, matching her in intensity, even though he believed himself to be with another.

""Yeah, Georgie, just like that. Take it all baby, it is all for you."

Not anymore, Marie smirked as she climbed that highest peak and came like an avalanche.

Something was horribly wrong. Beau hovered on the verge of consciousness, not quite willing to let the dream of his Georgie go. But since when had Georgie's hips been this narrow? Or that quiet? His woman loved loud and true, not at all like the mewing whimpers he was hearing. Warning bells in his head began to ring so loudly he could hear them in his ears. Yet, he could not stop the physiological need to release. As his balls tightened unbearably, his eyes opened slowly.

"What the hell!"

Regardless of the extreme pain in every muscle in his body, Beau literally threw the woman off him precious seconds before his release poured forth. Chest heaving, Beau tried to bank his rage, but this was too much! How many different ways did he have to tell this woman he didn't want her? What had she made him do?

"I don't know what the hell you think you were doing," he sneered through clinched teeth, "but do not ever touch me again. I don't want you. I don't mean to hurt your feelings, but I could never want you."

Marie's eyes widened as she fought to bring forth tears. She knew he would be upset, but he hadn't even apologized for throwing her to the floor! Although she was sprawled completely in the nude, there was nothing but fierce scalding anger in his eyes.

"*Monsieur*, I am so sorry. I saw you were in need," Marie shrugged and let out a small sniffle.

Beau was not in the least bit fooled by the huge crocodile tears flowing from her devious eyes. She wanted something from him, and he was not so arrogant to believe it was just *him*. She was trying too hard.

"You can either tell me what you're after, lady, or I'm walking out of here and I won't be back! Good luck trying to get your precious information or your brother out of France if I do because I promise you I will regretfully report that you were killed when my plane crashed right into you!"

"You wouldn't dare!" Surging to her feet, Marie forgot all about the demure lady she was pretending to be. "So it is true then, what Gilles and David think? You do not like women, eh?"

Beau's already hurting head began to pound against his skull. Was it all French women or just this one that was so damn crazy? Turning his back to her, he picked up the cold cloth inside an ever colder bowl of water to wash the remains of his release off of his stomach then stuffed himself back into his tattered pants. He wasn't about to have an argument with an insane woman with his dick hanging out. He didn't bother buttoning his shirt, it hurt too much to move around, plus she had already practically raped him, what was a little skin at this point?

Sitting down on the cart, he eyed the petite woman critically. She was actually quite pretty. A little on the small side, not standing over five feet, she had rich dark brown hair cut in a short bob. It suited her pixie like features. Her skin was clear and free of blemishes despite the harsh conditions of a war torn country. She should have no problems attracting a man. This sudden interest in him had begun when she learned he was not British, but American. There had been a light in her eyes that made him distinctly uncomfortable.

"No, I do *not* prefer men." He kept his voice low and even, looking directly in her eyes so she had no doubt he meant every word that came out of his mouth. "I prefer *my* woman. And you are not her by any stretch of the imagination. I would strongly advise you to never, ever do something like this again, or I will forget you are a woman. Now do you want to tell me what you are really after before I make good on my threat?"

Marie considered her options, none of them looking too good right now. If she told him the truth, what would he do? He seemed like an honorable man, would he help her and David, or would he walk away? It was worth the risk. She had a feeling this American would not leave her or her brother to an uncertain fate. He would help her; she could seduce him later. If he agreed, she would have plenty opportunities.

"I am a Jew, as is David, of course." She decided to take the direct route, discarding the false tears of pleading eyes. Apparently whoever this Georgie woman was, she never bothered using womanly arts on this man. The poor fool. "The German's are rounding my people up and putting them on trains. They say they are taking them to work camps, but no one ever hears from these people again. There are rumors…"

The fearful shudder that racked her body was real this time. Beau had heard the same rumors. The few that had escaped to England lived in constant fear. It was sickening to him that the English government sent many more back.

"How can I help you? My orders were to get David, not you." What had she been thinking to negotiate her brother's way out, but not her own? And what kind of man was David to let her?

"I want you to help me get out. Not just me, but David also. Gilles is not Jewish, he will be fine. But if David and I are caught we will be sent to the camps."

"How can I possibly get you out?" Beau was beyond exasperated. He couldn't force the British to take her and her brother. Hell, he wasn't even a citizen. "I can't force the British to take you or your brother."

"You can if you marry me."

Chapter Eight

Beau was nervous as he got off the train. He knew Georgie wouldn't be there, his father had written him as soon as he and his…entourage had landed in Washington D.C. He had been held up for a month with debriefings at the Pentagon about the growing threat the Germans posed. It seemed even if the lawmakers were claiming neutrality, the military was gearing up. Just in case they said, yet they wanted him to travel to Hawaii to train pilots. He just hoped there was enough time to warn them what to expect from the German pilots.

Germany had already declared war on the United States; the United States just chose to ignore it. Many in Europe were calling them cowards, not understanding the American isolationist mentality. Soon there would be no choice, of that Beau had no doubts.

He had a plan all worked out in his mind. He would return to Blakely for a month, then he and Georgie would travel to Hawaii. As for the others, well, his mother always wanted a daughter-in-law. Until he could secure a divorce, which was hard as hell in the South, he would leave Marie to her. Taking a deep breath, he got off the train to face his future.

Branford had once believed there was no deeper pain than the kind that was self-inflicted. He had been wrong. He hurt for his son; a soul deep anguish he could do nothing to heal. Looking at his son's expectant face, all he could do was shake his head sadly. Beau wanted understanding, he wanted his father to tell him it would be okay. Branford couldn't tell him that because it wouldn't be okay. Even if Georgie could forgive him for this, Beau would never forgive himself. Eventually, it would start eating at his soul. As grateful and happy as he was to have his boy back, Branford knew there would be very little happiness in Beau's immediate future. All he could do was pray that somehow, someway, Beau would work out this mess. He couldn't help him on this one.

Clasping his son to him, he whispered in his ear, "We need to talk, privately."

Nothing good was going to come from his father's tone. Nodding curtly, he turned back to introduce his mother to Marie.

"Momma, this is…This is Marie, uh, Dupuis." He couldn't call her his wife. She was no wife to him.

Lily Anne rushed forward, engulfing the slight French woman in a bear hug. Her vehemence shocked Beau. Lily Anne Dupuis was nothing if not perpetually cool no matter the situation. The older woman actually had tears in her eyes as she welcomed a beaming Marie to the family.

Beau couldn't take it. The sheer hypocrisy of it all. Bile rose fast and furious from his gut. He would not live a life like this. He couldn't. Everything inside him screamed for Georgie. He had to get to their home, to make sure she was alright and to make her understand. She would be furious for a while, but eventually, she would understand. She had to.

The ride to his parents' house was interminable. As much as he missed everything about Georgia, he stared out the window without seeing the lush green grass or majestic trees. He never noticed the magnolias in bloom, painting the landscape in delicate white, pinks, and yellows. All he could think about was Georgie.

How was he going to face her? How would he tell her? There was no way he could keep his marriage a secret. Hell half the town probably already knew. Would she yell and scream, or would she cry? Georgie was nothing if not naturally feisty. She would probably pop him upside his head, and he would deserve it. All he could do was hope that she would listen to his reasoning and give him time to get out of this mess. He would talk to his father immediately after reaching the house.

Branford had the best lawyers in all of the South. It was hard to get a divorce, but it wasn't impossible. In the meantime, he and Georgie would be in Hawaii, far away from Blakely and the laws that bound them. By the time the car drove up the path to his parents' house, Beau felt damn near hopeful. All he had to do was explain the situation to Georgie.

"Son, come into my study."

Beau was so caught up in visions of making up with his woman, he hadn't noticed he was standing in the foyer like an idiot, staring at nothing. He grimaced and followed his father, discreetly readjusting his pants to accommodate his growing erection. Damn, he needed to get to the house to see Georgie. His head pounded as his libido returned with vehemence. He hadn't had any interest in anything sexual since leaving Georgia. Why would he? Everything he had ever wanted was right here.

Although he had married Marie, he had not touched her. She had tried everything in her power to seduce him, not only in the bunker, but the entire time they had made their escape. The only way to be rescued by the British was to travel through the very heart of German-occupied France, through the Pyrenees Mountains to Spain, where they were finally rescued. The trip had taken months, and with his injuries, he had slowed them all down significantly. Marie had been right there, every step of the way. She had nursed him back to health when he had fallen ill with fever more than once during the arduous journey. The only way the British would agree to take her and her brother with them was if he married her. He had felt obligated. She had saved his life more than once.

That didn't mean he could bring himself to think of this as a real marriage. His heart was already married. Although Beau had explained that to Marie over and over again, she refused to hear it. She still crept in his bed at night, rubbing her body against his own. However, since that first time in the bunker, he couldn't get it up for her. Not for anyone woman. It had taken so damn long to break down Georgie's defenses, he couldn't let anything else come between them.

Ah, but you did you dolt, his conscious echoed through his head. *You got married. She will see that as proof you are everything she first believed you to be.*

No! He could not accept that. He needed Georgie like he needed air to breathe. Whatever he had to do to prove that to her, he would do. If he had to grovel at her feet, hell, he would do that too. Nothing in the world was more important. He understood that now more than ever.

Running off to fight a war that was not yet his to fight had been a fool thing to do. There was no doubt in Beau's mind the U.S. would eventually be dragged kicking and screaming into this thing, there was no way out of it with Germany literally trying to gobble up not only countries in Europe, but in Africa and Asia as well. Sooner or later, if Germany, or their Allies in Japan, Italy, and Spain didn't do something stupid, their worldwide power grab would start hitting Americans right in the pocket, and it wasn't like there was much give in anyone's pockets these days.

He should have waited. His own country would need him soon, and all he could do was teach others how to fight. His own hubris led him to run off to England, as if he could save them from the Germans single-handedly. Yeah, there was the letter begging for help, but no one would have blamed him for not going. It hadn't been his fight. He still felt it was a justified fight, but not his.

"Beau, I kind of need you here."

His father's rough voice brought Beau's snapping up, his eyes going to the man who seemed to have aged ten years since he had been gone. It must have been hard on him, on both his parents. The weight of his guilt increased tenfold, his shoulders dropping under the pressure. What an arrogant fool he had been.

"I know you probably want to high tail it out to the-your house."

There was something ominous in Branford's voice, something that made Beau's stomach drop to his feet. He didn't like it one bit. His father was looking down, refusing to meet his direct gaze, the older man's hands shaking ever so slightly as he leaned heavily against the desk. This would not be good news.

"Where is Georgie?" There was no point in beating around the bush. Beau's heart sped up so fast and hard, it felt like it wanted out of his chest. *Please, God, please don't let anything have happened to Georgie.*

"Georgie's not here."

Well, no shit. Beau had figured that much out. There was a hell of lot more to that simple statement, so he silently waited, allowing his father to feel the full force of his glare. Neither of them would be leaving this study until he found out exactly where his woman was. After that, well, he would be on his way to retrieve her.

"Why did you marry that French woman, Beau? What did you do?"

The old man's eyes shone with unshed tears, knocking Beau back so hard he had to sit heavily in one of the chairs placed in front of the desk. If Georgie already knew of his marriage, there was no telling how far away she was. There was no telling what she might have done by now. A woman who would walk for miles to keep from being his whore would not sit idly by while he brought home a wife.

Shit! She must have thought everything she feared had come true, that she would end up just like Ida. The pain ripping through Beau's body was a thousand times worse than when he had crashed. The room spun from the relentless hammering in his brain. He had to put his head down between his knees to pant for breath. The thought of Georgie, of her smile, her laugh, the way she purred when she was satisfied just like a cat, were all the things that spurred him when he wanted to give up hope and just lie down and die. He could give a damn about anything but that woman.

"She saved my life," Beau groaned through his anguish. "She couldn't stay in France. If she were caught…"

"Damn it, Beau! It is her country!" Branford thundered suddenly, the sound of his bellow slashing through the stillness of the room. His anger was so intense, Beau could feel vibrating in waves, beating at him in his guilt.

What have I done?

"She is a Jew," he whispered brokenly, trying to fight off the invisible fists of his father's anger. He knew Branford had supported taking Georgie as his own, now it was apparent Branford hadn't wanted his son in the situation he had found himself caught in. Who knew? All these years he had thought his father a hypocrite. He was twice the fool it seems. "The Germans are rounding them up, no one knows where they are sending them, but none of them are seen or heard from again. She saved my life. It was the least I could do."

Branford sank down in his chair, his body deflating as if someone had let out all the air in his lungs. "Damn."

The whispered word was worse than an indictment. Suddenly Beau wasn't so sure he wanted to know where she was, or who she was with. It might kill him.

"We had to send her to Louisiana," Branford ignored Beau's unspoken plea. "To New Orleans. She…I sent Ida with her. They are both in New Orleans right now."

Beau surged to his feet. "I am going to get her."

He didn't make a step before his father's voice stopped him cold.

"Beau-she knows you're married. She knows about Marie. I thought-Hell, I don't know what I thought.

"How the hell could you do that!" Beau thundered, blood rushing to his face to turn him crimson in his indignation. "You of all people! What were you trying to do? Get rid of her so there wouldn't be yet another Dupuis running around with a colored mistress and a passel of half-breed kids? How dare you judge me, her, us! I would NEVER do that to Georgie. I was going to beg you to help me get out of this travesty of a marriage, but you had to go and take matters into your own hands. You really are a hypocrite!"

"Georgie was pregnant when you left, Beau."

Branford didn't yell his proclamation, he didn't have to. His words, so softly delivered, slapped Beau to his knees. His chest heaved. Oh Lord, he couldn't breathe! Why hadn't she told him? She should have said something, anything.

"She knew it might have stopped you, and you would regret not going. Might even resent her. She didn't want that." Branford panted, gulping in air as if the pain his son felt he too shared. "Damn it, Beau you should have told me all of it. I just knew she didn't deserve to raise a child alone. She had plenty of suitors sniffin' around her skirts, at least that is what Ida says.

She deserved to have a father for her son. Beau, Georgie is engaged. She is to be married at the end of the week."

Over his dead and rotten corpse. Georgie was his. His son, oh Lord he had a son. And she had gone through it all alone, with no one but his father's mistress to care for her. Damn, damn, and double damn, he was beyond a fool.

"Why is she in New Orleans?" Branford had never said. She could have had the child here. She would have wanted that, Beau was sure of it.

"Lily."

Beau's eyes closed as he sank the rest of the way to the floor. What had he brought her to? He never should have dragged her anywhere near Dupuis land, or his twisted parents. *Oh, baby what have I done to you?* It couldn't be too late. It just couldn't be. If he had to crawl over hot coals, eat glass, anything, he had to get her back. But how could he like this? With a wife he never wanted and a mother as evil as the day was long. He should let her marry, walk away, and leave her alone, but he knew he couldn't do it.

"I need a lawyer, the best in the country," Beau whispered, his eyes still closed. It hurt too much to open them and face the world. "I will be leaving in the morning, and I won't be back."

Dragging his body up from the floor, Beau walked with leaden feet out of the study, and straight into a white-faced

Marie, clutching a handkerchief to her mouth. She said nothing, but silent tears made slow tracks down her face. Whatever false hopes she had harbored were well and truly crushed. There would be no marriage. He had tried to warn her.

"Beau Cantwell, I will not allow you to leave here after that-that-WHORE!" Lily screeched, grabbing for her son's arms.

Beau stared at the woman who had birthed him blankly. He should feel something he realized with detached wonder. Hate, love, pity. He felt none of it. He couldn't bring forth a single feeling, however faint. Life had been harsh to the once beautiful belle, but he would not pay the price for that.

"What is wrong with you?" Lily demanded, sneering first at her son, then her husband. "It is a sickness. A dark demon in both your souls! It is a crime against nature and against God! You are possessed to lust after demons! You will be damned if you leave this house, Beau Cantwell! I have done my Christian duty, you walk away from this lovely woman God has seen fit to bless you with despite your evil wicked soul, and you are no longer my son!"

The laugh that emitted from Beau had nothing to do with joy. No longer her son? Did she believe that to be some kind of threat?

"Madame, I would gladly claim the Whore of Babylon for a mother before recognizing you ever again." It was cruel, it was ungentlemanly, but that was the way he felt. He had no patience for this woman and her bitterness. It had turned into something far more evil than she believed Georgie or Ida to be. Shaking his head, he walked towards the stair to retrieve his luggage. He wouldn't be staying here another minute. "And the daughter-in-law you are so happy with is a Jew," he threw over his shoulder.

No one bothered to even try to catch Lily as she sank into a dead faint.

Chapter Nine

"Don't you look the picture?" Ida gushed as she hemmed the ivory and lace colored wedding gown.

A picture of what? Abject misery? Try as she might, Georgie just couldn't work up any kind of enthusiasm for her upcoming nuptials. Lucien Roux was a godsend. He had begun his courtship when she was pregnant, ignoring the disapproving frowns of many of the Creole matrons to whose community he belonged. He escorted her to the market, came to sit with her when she couldn't get around so easily anymore, brought her flowers after she gave birth.

It had been wrong to encourage Lucien. She had been so damn lonely, even with Ida here to keep her company. Branford Dupuis traveled here often enough to see if she needed anything, but Georgie wasn't fooled. It wasn't her he was coming to see. The sounds of his reunion with Ida mocked her late at night.

She felt as if she was missing a piece of herself every day Beau was gone, maybe even a piece of her soul. Lord, how she missed Beau. She prayed with every fiber of her being every night for his safe return.

When had she come to depend so deeply on Beau? She had been so very determined to have a respectable life. She had such plans. Maybe not grand ones, but plans nonetheless. Beau had waltzed right into her life and took it for a tailspin. She never knew she could travel to such heights, or plunge to such depths.

Inhaling deeply, Georgie forcibly fought back the sting of tears gathering in her eyes. How could he do this to her? How could she have believed in him? She was a fool. She had known where their relationship was heading. She was a complete idiot to believe otherwise. But oh, how she had wanted to believe in Beau. His smile could brighten a gray, stormy day. His hands, his mouth, his loving could make her speak in tongues. Even now, knowing he was married to a nice, respectable white woman as was expected of him, her body still ached in remembrance of his touch. Her core still throbbed at the thought of him. It yearned for him, burned for him.

Oh, Beau how could you?

A piercing wail broke through her morose thoughts. Making her excuses to Ida, Georgie shrugged of the gown that had come to symbolize a chain to her. It would chain her to a man she didn't love for the sake of the child she would die for. Rushing over to the bassinet in the corner of the room, Georgie lifted her son, cradling him close.

Bright blue eyes blinked up at her, a startling contrast to his café au laît skin. It amazed her how every time she looked at him, a fresh wave of awe swept through her like a tidal wave.

So tiny, so perfect. He didn't deserve to live his life constantly punished for his mother's sins. For him, she would brave anything, even being condemned to live the rest of her life without love.

No matter what Beau had done, this child had been conceived in love. Yes, Beau had hurt her, ripped her heart apart, and thrown it on the floor to be stomped on some more. But Georgie knew the joy she had found in his arms had been real. Every second they had been together was real. It was a foolish dream, one that could have never amounted to anything more than stolen moments, but it had been real. And Beau in his selfish arrogance had loved her. Probably, in his own way, he still did. However, Georgie could not afford that kind of love.

She didn't regret it. Not a single second. Had she succeeded in her plans to marry the first dirt sharecropper who asked, she would have lived a miserable existence, albeit an honest one. So dead set in being respectable, she would have known what it was like to burn with the sacred fire only love could ignite.

Settling into the rocker, she shifted the baby so she could nurse him. He was eight months old and had begun to eat mashed food, but she took joy in nursing him. She would have to quit soon, she knew, but she was determined to enjoy every second she could being this close to her son. It gave her such a sense of completeness to know at least part of his nourishment came from her. It made her feel like the most accomplished person in the world.

Humming a wordless tune, she rocked her precious bundle, shutting out all the cares of the world as her universe dissolved and refocused on one single being.

"It's true. I have a child."

Georgie's blood froze in her veins even as her skin blazed with righteous anger. She didn't know why she was so shocked to see him; of course, his father had told him about the baby. She had no idea why she had convinced herself otherwise. *Like father, like son*, she thought scornfully, trying to screw up her courage to do what she knew she had to do. Bitterness threatened to choke her as he stood there, staring at the baby on her arms. The sour bile of her anger rose like a volcano.

Damn it! He had no right! He had no right to be here, no right to seek her out, and he damn sure didn't have any right to her son! While he was out trying to save the world, she was the one waiting patiently for his return, growing ever heavier with his child. He was off having a grand adventure while she labored, hour after hour, feeling as if she was being ripped apart from the inside, bringing that child into the world. While he was racing across France to get to Spain, she was pacing the floors with a screaming infant alone, whispering to him his father would be coming home soon, his father would be so happy to meet him. He had caused her to lie to her son.

The fact remained she was the only parent her baby had ever known. That made him hers and hers alone.

"You can just turn right back around and go home to your wife."

Her voice vibrated, her anger coming through loud and clear. Thank the Good Lord for that. She didn't want to show him a speck of her pain; he didn't deserve to see it. Plus, she didn't want to upset the baby as he nursed.

"Georgie, baby, I swear I didn't know."

Georgie tried to be unmoved by the anguish showcased in his voice. Regret liberally laced every syllable, making him sound broken, defeated. She had never seen Beau anything but confident, if not a bit cocky. It was unnerving. Heavy lines framed his eyes and mouth, his dark hair sprinkled with gray. Even his posture, which had always been so erect, so strong and confident seemed a bit bent inward, though his spine was as straight as ever. Beau looked…haggard.

Her heart cried out by instinct. Having known him better than anyone else on earth, she could tell he had suffered. How deeply she probably would never know. Her arms twitched, wanted so badly to encase him, to smother him in her embrace, to whisper encouragement in his ears and chase those shadows far from his eyes. She squashed those feelings ruthlessly.

She could not afford to give an inch. Beau would take a mile. She knew she wouldn't be strong enough to withstand the storm that would be brought on by his touch, his kiss, his honey smooth lies. She would find herself raising her son in a little house abutting his father's bigger home that he shared with his "respectable" family, his white family. As much as Georgie had grown to like and respect Ida, she could not live the older woman's life. For one thing, Ida had a husband that afforded her the veneer of respectability, however rusty that veneer was. And as deep as the love obviously was between Ida and Branford, Georgie could not stomach being the other woman, the colored mistress. She damned sure couldn't take sharing her man with someone with the legal rights to him.

"Will you just let me explain?"

Georgie had never heard desperation in Beau's voice before. Not like this. He had been aggressive in his courtship, such as it was. He had begged and pleaded, pulling out every stop in the book. He had seduced her mind and body. Even after she had returned to the house with him after attempting to return to her father's he had never stopped in his pursuit of her love. But he had never been so despondent, so frantic to get her to listen.

That only solidified her resolve not to hear it. She would be hopping mad one minute and melting the next, worried about *his* feelings. Beau was unconsciously selfish that way. He didn't set out to deliberately hurt anyone, kind of like a storm doesn't deliberately set out to ruin home and fields. There was probably a very good reason he returned to the States with a wife in tow, but she didn't need to hear it. It wouldn't change her situation or heal her broken heart.

"No. I am going upstairs to change *my* child. Please don't be here when I come back down."

She waltzed out of the room, head held as regal as a queen. She had almost made it to the staircase when his voice stopped her cold.

"Please, can I just hold him? Just once, Georgie. He is the only child I will ever have."

The tears in his voice almost made her knees buckle. Almost. She did not turn around, seeing evidence of the sob in his words would destroy her. It had taken too much to pull herself back together as it was.

"Nothing good can come of it. Go, Beau. Forget we exist. It is easier for…everyone."

*****

He watched her go, her back ramrod straight, never once turning around. The sound of every footfall was like the sound of someone nailing his coffin. Rubbing his chest to attempt to ease the piercing ache, he walked blindly into the room she had just vacated, standing over the whitewashed cradle. He should leave. That's what she wanted. But Lord, help him he could not make his feet turn around and head to the door.

What have I done?

Beau knew without having to contemplate the question. He had destroyed her faith in him. He had broken his word. Most of all, he hurt the person he loved more than life itself.

So, let her go.

The pain knocked him to his knees. Clutching the cradle where his child had so recently lain, he rested his head against the warm wood, gulping in air like a man drowning. Without Georgie, there was nothing. Nothing. Had Marie's life been worth this? What kind of a man even asked that question?

"Damn it all to hell!" The roar shook the stillness of the room, but from the staircase there was not a sound.

"She is supposed to get married tomorrow."

Ida's voice didn't inspire him to move, but he did listen.

"I never said anything because it's not my place," the older woman went on. "But that man, he is no good. Gambler and a drunkard. Careful enough to hide it from her, but people ain't so cautious around me."

Beau lifted his head, his eyes bright with the sheen of his unshed tears. The tiny flame of hope that had almost been washed away in despair sputtered to life.

"I will go and get the baby," Ida told him moving away towards the stairs. "You go on up there and get your woman."

"She doesn't want me."

As much as he wanted to believe otherwise, she had shown no softening, no forgiveness.

Why should she? He had failed her. Not so much by marrying Marie. No matter how much he disliked her as a person, Marie had saved his life. Nevertheless, he had placed himself in that circumstance. At the very least, he should have taken Georgie to Canada and married her first. He should have never gone. It didn't matter that he had meant everything he had ever told her before he left. His actions had made a lie of his well-intentioned words. They were now worth no more than sawdust.

"Make it right, Beau," Ida whispered fiercely. "She doesn't deserve a life chained to a fool. Make it right."

A plan formulated in his mind before Ida had made another step. "Ida, wait!"

He would need her help, as well as the help of his father, but it could be done.

"You need to get upstairs, Beau!"

"No, not yet. Georgie needs a little space right now." She needed to cool off. Plus, she needed to get over the shock of him standing in her doorway. And he needed to get prepared. "And, I am going to need your help."

Chapter Ten

She was going to vomit. As soon as Georgie opened her red rimmed eyes, she knew there was no way she could go through with the wedding today. Seeing Beau again, witnessing how badly he had been affected by the war and his impromptu marriage, she just couldn't do it. She would never return to Georgia, probably would never see the man she loved more than air ever again, but she wouldn't be trapped in a loveless marriage. It would only exasperate all the hurt and betrayal. She would end up blaming Beau for her own stupid reactionary mistake and end up hating him.

She didn't want to hate Beau. He may have hurt her so bad it hurt to breathe, but she didn't hate him. She wished she did. It would be so much easier if she could slam the door on her wayward emotions, lock away the ever yearning of her heart and body, if she could just hate him a little. "In the months she had spent lying in his arms, listening to his dreams of running away and building an impossible future that only included the two of them, Georgie had grown to know Beau like nobody else could. He believed those dreams of his. He hadn't been lying to her, as much as she wanted to paint him that way.

Beau was not deliberately selfish or reckless. He was a product of his upbringing. The only legitimate child of a magnate, he had never learned there were things in life he just couldn't have. No one said no to Beau Dupuis. No one dared. As a result, he simply took what he wanted, including her. He may have had to wait patiently, lay careful groundwork for his ultimate siege, but he knew in the end he would have her. And so had she, no matter how she might have professed otherwise.

Something had happened in France. She knew he had been shot down, and this marriage happened afterwards, when he was trying to escape. There was probably a very good explanation. The problem was she could care less about that explanation. Well, she could have cared less before seeing him. His eyes told a story her ears didn't want to hear. She didn't want to know the reasonable excuse for bringing home a wife. She wanted to hold on to her anger. By holding on, she could use that hurt to push him away. If she let go, she would just fall back into his arms and become the whore all the nosey, bitter women in Blakely had always declared her to be.

She couldn't go back there and face the smug "I told you so" looks and vicious whispers. She was tired to death of the gossip that followed her. Only this time, the gossip would not be about things she had no control over, rather what she had willingly done. She would be judged, and judged harshly, and she refused to face that.

A sharp knock on the bedroom door got her out of the bed and out of her useless mental meanderings. There was no point. She had sent Beau away. He was probably halfway to Georgia by now.

Shrugging into her robe she opened the door without looking, then turned to gather up the baby. Ida was supposed to come take him while she prepared for the wedding. Well, there would be no wedding, but she still had to hurry and dress to catch Lucien before he left for the church. She had to call this thing off before it was too late.

"I need to run out for a minute, Ida," Georgie threw over her should while rushing toward the wardrobe. "I have to catch Lucien before he leaves for the church."

"Why, Georgie? Don't you know it's bad luck for a groom to see his bride before the wedding?"

She froze where she stood. So, he hadn't left. She was so sure he would. He looked so resigned yesterday. But then, that was her Beau.

No, not her Beau. He was his wife's. She had to remember that, she had to hold on to that like a talisman against the coming storm because that was her only hope of keeping him away.

"Get out!" she screamed, forgetting the baby sleeping peacefully in his cradle.

As soon as the screech left her lips, the baby wailed in protest. Changing direction, Georgie ran to her child, suddenly terrified Beau might do so. It was silly really, Beau already knew the baby was his. Still, as long as she could keep him from touching the child, from seeing him up close, she could pretend he didn't know. That he wasn't the least bit interested. Another shield to guard her heart, but she was looking for any excuse at this point.

Casting a withering, but quick, look over her shoulder, she loosened her gown in front to feed the baby. There was no way in hell she was going to let him see her feeding, so she pulled a light blanket over her should to drape the sight from Beau as she sank into the rocker next to the cradle.

Inhaling a shaky breath, she observed Beau through the thick fan of her lashes. He looked somewhat better than he had last night, but he still had a tired, worn air about him. Still, a spark was there now that wasn't the night before; a new light brightened his cobalt eyes that made her immediately wary. He was up to something.

Despite the limp that made her heart bleed, he strode toward her with definite purpose. She was not about to cower, even though her heart tripped in her chest. There was just something about a determined Beau that was damned sexy — a ghost of the old Beau, resolute, indomitable, a man who got what he wanted.

He is the husband of another, you can't give in.

She didn't try to stop him as he lifted the blanket off her chest and shoulder because she was mesmerized by the awe freezing his face in a slack-jawed gape. She could see his fingers trembling as he traced the delicate skin of the baby's face. Georgie saw the shimmer of tears she had never thought to see such a strong man shed as he looked at the tiny image of his very own face. The same blue eyes stared back at Beau in an unwavering, unblinking stare, as each was fascinated by what they were beholding for the very first time.

"What is his name?" His voice choked, as if he could hold back the emotions that were so clear to her.

He loved him. He loved their child every bit as much as she did. It was written all over his face, and not even in her bitterest hour could she deny it with any degree of honesty.

"His name is Beau."

*****

It hurt. It hurt so bad he should have been bleeding. He should be able to look down and see his chest ripped to shreds. He was the most beautiful thing Beau had ever seen. So innocent, so fragile, and he had left Georgie to bringing this miracle into the world alone.

Oh, Lord, he was such an ass. It had seemed so important to go and fight at the time. He had felt a duty. What a stupid fool he had been. His duty was right here, lying the arms of the woman he loved more than life itself.

And he had hurt her. He had taken her love and her trust and stomped right over them, then came home expecting…what? For Georgie to just open her arms at his simplistic explanation? There was no excuse good enough for what he had done. His hand in marriage hadn't been his to give, and yet he threw it away. He didn't deserve Georgie's love. He didn't deserve to be a father to this beautiful child in her arms.

Still, he could let her, them, go.

"I don't deserve your forgiveness, Georgie," Beau whispered, slipping to his knees at her feet. "But I beg you for it. I will work every day of my life to be worthy of you. I swear."

It wasn't good enough; nothing would be good enough. His daddy had always told him men didn't cry. That may be so, but he didn't even try to hold back the stinking tears in his eyes. He had never felt so helpless. There had never been any cause for him to. All his life he had been the master of all he surveyed. There was nothing he could do to master this.

Georgie's hurt was a tangible thing, beating him upside the head in sharp shards. She didn't try to move him as he lay at her feet, his head resting pitifully on his knee, but he could feel the tension in her body. He couldn't soothe her. He couldn't take it back or make it go away.

He had come here with the express purpose of seducing her back into his arms. Last night, he had tracked down her so-called fiancé, Lucien. The man had been spending the night before his marriage at a poker game in a cathouse in Storyville, and he had been losing badly.

Beau had been prepared to threaten, to cajole, to do anything under the sun to get him to disappear. Turns out all he had to do was pay the man off. Thinking about it now made him feel worse. She deserved so much more than a degenerate gambler or a spoiled rich boy.

And that was just what he was. A spoiled rich boy. He had seen her, wanted her, and he took her. Good intentions aside, he had damn near broken her.

"I have to go."

Beau raised his head, but he did not move. How was he supposed to tell her there would be no groom waiting at the altar? Though the only people that were supposed to be present were her, the groom, the baby, and Ida, she would be mortified to be left alone standing in front of the preacher.

"Please, Georgie, please don't do this," all he could do was beg.

He couldn't tell her what he'd done. All she had wanted her entire life was respectability. He had taken that option away from her—again.

Georgie sighed heavily, shaking her head mournfully. She looked like the weight of the world had settled firmly on her shoulders. The tear in his chest widened, leaving a gaping hole in its wake. He couldn't keep doing this to her. He was only making it worse.

He was going to have to leave her alone. Oh, Lord, he was going to have to walk away.

Beau was so startled by his own thoughts, he stumbled backward, falling on his behind in the process. His eyes stretched wide in disbelief. Surely, that wasn't the only way to make it right? There had to be something else! He just had to think of something. He father would find away to procure him a divorce, surely it couldn't be that hard.

Yeah, your daddy can make it all better, his formerly dormant conscious screamed into the white noise in his brain.

He created this mess, and he had to clean it up.

"Give me three months," Beau pleaded without getting up. He voice projected all the desperation he felt to his bones. She was slipping away, sliding through his hands like it had all been nothing but a fanciful dream. "I swear, I will make this right. Georgie, I can't breathe without you."

"I have no intention of marrying Lucien," Georgie sighed, rising from her chair and stepping over his prone body. "But I have no intention of taking you back either."

With that, she calmly left the room.

No histrionics, no cussing, no crying. Just a calmly spoken statement. They both knew this would not be the end of it, but the words didn't fail to chill Beau to his very soul. It was a challenge he was going to have to meet. Georgie would not settle this time, and she would not wait until Beau could figure out a "perfect plan." If he wanted to be a part of her life, of their son's life, he was going to have to do it right.

Chapter Eleven

"When are you gonna forgive that boy?"

Georgie shook her head as she resumed refolding the laundry. It was not a task she had to do. The laundry service they used did a good enough job. However, whenever Beau was here visiting their son, she had to keep her hands busy and stay well away. There simply weren't enough chores around the sprawling house located in Faubourg Marigny, not far from the Quarter. The neighborhood was on the decline, not many people had money for the upkeep of houses originally built for the colored mistresses of rich white Creoles and Anglophones who wanted to pretend they were descendants of the original Franco-Spanish Creoles.

It was a bitter irony that Branford had settled his son's whore here, Georgie snorted. Not that she blamed him. Had she lived in East New Orleans or the scarcely populated 9th Ward, there would be questions as soon as her son was born.

Uncomfortable questions and even more uncomfortable looks. There may well be plenty of interesting combinations in the people of the Big Easy, but the social mores remained the same.

"He made his bed," was the only answer she had for Ida.

Of all the people in the world, she had thought Ida would understand her feelings. She had seen the sadness in the other woman's eyes every time Branford breezed in and out of town. She saw the tightening of Ida's hands whenever Branford packed his bags to return to his wife and his respectable life. How could she try to push Georgie into such a life? At least Ida had the thin veneer of respectability. She was married.

If Beau thought for a second she was going to marry one of his illegitimate brothers, he had another damn thing coming. There was no way she could live Ida's life. The degradation would be galling.

"Now that slick Creole is gone, you need to think about Little Beau," Ida huffed as she snapped peas in a large pot. "The boy needs a father."

"Like Branford was a father to your children?" Georgie snapped before she thought the better of it.

As soon as the words flew out of her mouth, Georgie was immediately shamed. That wasn't fair. Ida hadn't had many choices in life. In his way, Branford *had* provided for her children. They had far, far more than any other colored children in Blakely could ever claim. Each had moved as far away from

Blakely as they could as fast as they could, leaving their mother to her lot in life. They had taken their daddy's money and ran, but at least they could run.

Ida did not respond. Her hands stilled over the pot as she struggled to compose her face. She didn't shed a tear, but Georgie could tell her words had been like a body shot straight to the gut.

"It's easy to cast stones, Georgina," Ida's voice was a broken whisper, a mixture of sadness and anger lacing each carefully pronounced word. "And it's easy to make that boy suffer. What is hard is raising that little boy of yours on your own, without somebody buying you a house to raise him in, or giving you the money to feed him." Ida shook her head as she placed the pot on the kitchen table. "You know, that boy loves you."

Georgie opened her mouth to protest, to tell Ida just what "that boy's" love had done to her, but Ida held up her hand.

"I know he done you wrong," the older woman told her. "There ain't no doubt about that. But I know that life ain't easy for any of us. You could sell yourself for a wedding ring and the approval of sour people who ain't never done a damn thing for you. You could live the rest of your life bitter, never again knowing the touch of a lover." Ida sighed as she rose from the chair, every one of her years in every step she took toward the door. She turned and looked sadly as Georgie. "Girl, I know your life hasn't been easy. I know he was wrong. But give him a chance to make it right. He ain't his daddy. He aint-"

Whatever Ida was going to say was abruptly halted as the older woman grasped at her chest.

Georgie dropped the clothes in her hands, rushing to the older woman to catch her just as she crumbled.

"Beau! Beau, come quick!"

Georgie ripped the top of Ida's dress open, trying to will the older woman to breathe. Even so, she could see Ida struggling, her mouth opening and closing, grunting in an attempt to say something.

"Oh, Lord, Ida I am so sorry." Georgie's tears dropped onto the face of the jerking woman in her arms faster than she could wipe them away. She didn't know what to do. Had her harsh words done this? "Ida, please, please…"

Ida managed to grab Georgie's dress near her chest, dragging her down closer with surprising strength. "Forgive him, Georgie. Promise me."

The words were barely audible, but she couldn't pretend she didn't hear them. She wanted to deny them, to push them away like she'd never heard them. But how could she do that?

"Promise me, Georgiana!" the fading croak of a voice demanded. "Let him make this right."

"I promise," she managed to whisper through her sobs. "Just please, fight!"

Unfortunately, her plea was too late. Ida sank into unconsciousness.

*****

Despite the emerald, mint, and forests greens of the landscape, the air held a decisive bite. The slate gray of the overcast sky matched the mood of those who rode silently in the car from the graveyard. No one spoke, there was really nothing to say. Each person was left to his or her own thoughts and remembrances. None willing to share their private pain.

"Are you certain you have to leave for Hawaii tomorrow?" Lily finally spoke as the black-clad group alighted from the car to take the long slow walk up the house stairs. "There is so much to do here. I am going to need your help cleaning things up around here."

Beau paused, sending his mother a curious glance. He couldn't shake the feeling that Lily was somehow relieved. She had held herself rigidly erect throughout the service, her eyes dry as a bone. Not that he had expected anything less. There had been no love lost between Lily and the deceased.

"I can't imagine you need my help with anything." He couldn't help his acidic tone. The last week had been hell. She hadn't said anything about his refusal to stay in her home, choosing to stay out at the house he used to share with Georgie, even if he had to sleep in the extra bedroom. Hell, he didn't deserve to sleep in Georgie's bed. Not yet.

"I don't want to discuss it out on the front steps," Lily sniffed. "Come into the front parlor, we can share some tea."

Beau inclined his head towards his mother's general direction. "After I have a word with my…wife in Daddy's study."

Marie's red-rimmed eyes swung to him in a mixture of hope and dread. He hated the wave of guilt that assaulted him, but he would not be deterred. This must be done, the sooner the better.

"Really, Beau," Lily sniffed. "Your father is good and dead. It is your study now."

There was no mourning apparent in Lily's voice. There was no sadness harbored in her eyes. Beau felt physically ill as he watched her turn on her heel and glide into the huge, cold, white house. The column gleaned in the weak sunlight, the red door a bright beacon. There was no welcome in the perfect façade, just the ghosts of bitter regrets and hypocrisy.

"So kind of you to remind me of the loss of the man I loved dearly, Madame," Beau drawled as unflappably as Lily's pronouncement.

Lily paused at the head of the stairs, but did not turn.

So be it. Beau had had enough. The place he had loved so dearly had turned into nothing but a symbol of acrimonious feelings and blind duplicity. This was not how he would live his life. He was done giving Lily, and those like her, the benefit of the doubt. He was finished with the excuses and the delicacy. Blakely held nothing for him; it was time for his life to begin.

Closing the study door behind Marie, Beau moved behind his father's massive Brazilian Rosewood desk. Tomorrow, movers would come to take this desk, and everything else in this house that had been his father's away. There was no way in hell he would allow Lily any part of the deceased Branford Dupuis. She had his name; she would have this house and the lands here in Georgia. She didn't deserve anything else.

There was no evidence there had been any foul play in his father's death. Still, the circumstances had been highly suspicious. Everyone who had seen his father on the day of his fatal heart attack had sworn he had been hale and hardy. In fact, most declared he had looked better than he had since before Beau went off to fight for the English. He had come home to a dinner prepared by Lily herself. He had the heart attack at the dinner table, at the exact moment Ida had experienced the symptoms in New Orleans.

Ida was fine, it hadn't been her heart. It had been his father's. There could not have been a greater testament to their love for each other than that strange, yet oddly poetic moment.

Beau wouldn't have been suspicious, if it wasn't for what his father had managed to accomplished earlier that day. Lily had known what Branford was working on, what she didn't know was that he had completed his mission. Perhaps she had thought to stop what had to be done. Maybe she thought getting rid of Branford would force Beau to stay here. He had many suspicions, but no answers.

"I am so sorry, Beau. We were eating, and your papa, he just…" Marie shook her head as a delicate shiver racked her body.

Beau watched her as if he were completely detached from his body. The sensation was peculiar, almost like he was peeking in a window at some melodrama unfolding.

"Sign these." Pushing a packet of papers toward her, he knew damn well she couldn't read English very well. It was duplicitous, but so very necessary. Marie had clung to his side every chance she got since he had returned here. He had returned to Georgia to find his "wife" was quite the southern belle. Long gone was the hardnosed, determined underground fighter he had known in France. Lily had succeeded in turning Marie into quite the lady. Bully for the two of them.

"But, what is this?" Funny how her accent returned and deepened whenever she addressed him. He supposed she thought men found it sexy. Most probably did.

"It is for your citizenship," was all he was willing to say. At least until she signed them.

"They came fast, non?" She was all smiles now, signing the papers without thinking to inspect them further.

Perfect. Just as he had intended.

As soon as all the papers were signed, Beau snatched them up, placing them in a portfolio that would not leave his side until he was well away from Blakely, Georgia.

"If you have a moment," Marie hedged, "I know you have to speak with you *maman*, but I would like to ask…I would like to know, if you will be in Hawaii for very long?"

Beau leaned back in his father's chair. He knew what was coming; he decided to let it ride. It was cruel perhaps, Marie had saved his life. But since she had been here, she had acted as if they hadn't had an agreement; he would marry her and bring her to the States, just as long as she gave him his freedom once she became a citizen. Once she was here, she had attempted to entrench herself in his parent's home and the community as his wife. That was not what they had agreed to and he resented the hell out of her for doing it.

If that wasn't bad enough, she had tried her damnedest to get him into bed. She rubbed against him every chance she got, and she tried to cajole him out of the earshot of his mother to stay the night with her. Last night she had gone so far as to beg, daring to bring up the fact he needed a son to carry on his father's name. She knew Georgie was out at the house down the lane, taking care of his son, yet she dismissed it, adopting the culture of the South whole-heartedly. As if he was ever going to change his mind, the idea was now abhorrent to him.

"I will be in Hawaii for quite a while," he drawled, offering no more information than that.

Marie cast puppy dog eyes at him, her lips in full pout. "I would like very much to come to see you. I mean, once we make sure your *maman* is okay of course."

Of course.

"Why would you want to do that?" Beau led her into the trap. He wanted her to say it so he could make sure she understood the situation for once and for all.

"I am your wife!" she had the audacity to look innocent and bewildered at his question. "It is my job to support you. You cannot think to take your…"

"Don't even think about completing that sentence," he warned in a deceptively mild tone. Anger engulfed him like a tidal wave. He wasn't sure what he would do if she dared.

"Beau," Marie sighed leaning forward to clasp his hand. "Your *maman*, she explained these things to me. You are a man, *non*? We French are not so uptight. I understand your little plaything. But surely you will want a proper wife to entertain for you? To give you, how do you say, respectable children, *oui*?"

"My son is perfectly respectable," he was clinching his teeth now, willing his temper to simmer down.

"He is not white! I am your wife! You-"

"You are not my wife," Beau told her coldly. "You are a United States citizen, perhaps a paid companion to my mother. But as of two minutes ago, you ceased being married to me."

He didn't wait for the words to sink in, but strode out of the study, leaving her gaping after him.

One down, one to go.

Now to take care of his mother. Then, finally, he would be free.

Chapter Twelve

He really wanted to tell her, but he wasn't ready to. Not yet. Beau entered the house that held such bittersweet memories for him with renewed purpose. Georgie and Ida were sitting in the kitchen, feeding Little Beau. Well, Georgie was feeding him while Ida stared off in the distance.

The robust woman seemed to have shrunk before their very eyes. Although she had never, ever shown it in public, Ida had loved Branford deeply. His death had been a cruel shock. The woman he had known growing up was becoming a ghost of her former self, rarely smiling at anything other than Little Beau. It was almost as if the inner light that had always shined so brightly within her was extinguished.

There was no way Beau could allow her to stay here. Lily would no doubt fire her as soon as Beau was gone. Suspecting as he did that Lily had killed his father, it was a fair bet she would try something horrific against Ida.

"Ida, may I talk to you for a few minutes?"

Georgie jumped at the sound of his voice, spinning around to face him. He wished so much he could gather her in his arms to apologize for startling her, but she wouldn't appreciate the gesture. Although she had been kind since learning of his father's death, she still allowed no physical contact between them.

Well, that would be changing soon.

They were moving to Hawaii; Georgie, Little Beau, Ida, himself would soon be making a brand new start on the tiny American territory. A little research and Beau had learned he and Georgie could marry there. No one thought to outlaw miscegenation on the tropical islands. Beau had agreed to train pilots for the Navy and the Army. Both had bases there.

It seemed that although most of the country was against it, the powers that be in Washington knew that war with Germany and their allies was inevitable. The government wanted to be prepared. Beau would not be an official member of the Armed Services, he was merely acting as a contractor of sorts. He had flown against the Germans. So, he had more than a little knowledge about how they operated.

Searching the face of the woman who he loved more than life, he knew he had made the right decision. They could have gone to Canada, but this way he could serve his country in some small way while being able to marry the woman he wanted to spend the rest of his life with.

At first, the Pentagon had wanted to send him to Mississippi, but there was no way in hell he was going to subject Georgie to the attitudes of the people there. It would be just like Blakely, only thousands of times worse. Nothing was more important to him than making things right with Georgie, absolutely nothing. He had been immoveable when the brass had tried to pressure him, claiming he owed it to the nation to help prepare young pilots for the coming battles. Maybe he did; he had after all flown to help another country fight. He had a certain responsibility to his own country.

It was nothing compared to the responsibility sitting around the kitchen table. He owed each one of them much more than he owed anything else. He would personally cheerfully walk on hot coals to diminish the sadness in Georgie's eyes. He would give all he owned to be a real father to his son, to have that son carry his name. It would happen. He'd move heaven and earth to make it so.

As Ida shuffled out of the kitchen, he mentally made a list of the final things he needed to accomplish before they could leave. First, he had to find an appropriate home, one with lots of space for more children should Georgie find it in her heart to give him another chance. He had to make sure he transferred plenty of assets into Georgie's name. He had almost died once without making sure she would be well taken care of. That could not ever happen again.

"Yes?" Ida asked quietly as they sat on the rockers on the porch.

Her voice sounded so tired and deflated. He wished there was something he could say to make it better, but he knew there was nothing that would. As much as he missed his father, he knew Ida missed him more. He wouldn't be able to survive without Georgie; he considered it a minor miracle Ida was able to breathe.

"We are moving," he told her quietly. He didn't want Georgie to know just yet. "I am taking Georgie and Little Beau to Hawaii. I want you to come with us."

A single tear escaped the weary eyes as she sadly shook her head.

"You don't have to do that," she insisted. "My life is right here. I can't leave."

He knew she would say that. He also knew he could not leave her here.

"Please, Ida," he implored. "We need you. Georgie will need you. Then there is Little Beau."

It was low to use the baby to twist her arm, but he would do and say whatever he had to.

Ida sighed heavily, looking out over the fields. He had her. He knew he did.

"Does Georgie know what you're planning?" Ida finally sighed after several minutes.

"I was hoping you could help me convince her," he teased.

It was true, he would need her help. There was no doubt he would have to resort to using the baby as an argument to get her to agree, just like he had with Ida. He wasn't above it. The most important thing was getting her there. Then maybe, hopefully, they could become a true family.

"Beau Cantwell Dupuis, you are a little devil."

There was the Ida he knew and loved. Her smile might be sad, but light had come back into her eyes.

"I can't deny it," he agreed. "Now here is what we are going to do."

Chapter Thirteen

Georgie chewed on her bottom lip, her hands knotting a handkerchief in her hands. Ida held Little Beau tightly as the private DC-3 descended back to earth. All in all, her first plane ride hadn't been so bad. She had been scared as all get out when she had boarded, but Beau had held her hand throughout the long flight, talking to her in low, soothing tones. She had no idea what he had said, she suspected he wasn't saying anything much at all, but his presence had soothed her.

Beau had changed since the death of his father. There was something much more determined, almost ruthless about him. She had no idea what had happened in the big house after the funeral, but when he had came back to the house they had formerly shared as lovers, he seemed to have banished the black cloud that had surrounded him since his return from Europe. And he watched her, watched her with an intensity that secretly thrilled her as much as it frightened her. She would not be able to withstand a concentrated campaign on his part to get her back into his bed. She was weak for Beau in general, but this new Beau was something to behold. Coupled with Ida's insistence she forgive him, especially now that he had lost his father, Georgie felt herself growing weaker and weaker with each passing day.

That was why she was here now with him. He hadn't taken no for an answer. Her other alternatives were to return to New Orleans with Ida, or drag her son and the older woman to some unknown destination. She certainly had the money to do that now. Branford had left both Georgie and Ida a nice nest egg, and even placed money in trust for Little Beau. The number had astounded her. Little Beau might have been his grandchild, but he was not a grandchild Branford could proudly place on his shoulders and brag to his friends about.

Moving back to her father's place was not an option. Georgie had long since forgiven him for basically selling her to Beau, but she could not condone it. What if it happened again? To give himself comfort, believing he was taking care of her and her child, would he do the same thing with some other unknown man? Maybe it wasn't fair to think about her father that way, but damn it she couldn't help it. He had sold her to Beau to soothe his own conscious about the way he raised her. Who knew what bee he would get in his bonnet next.

Georgie had to think not only about Little Beau, but also Ida. Branford had been Ida's world. When she had collapsed, Georgie had been so afraid. Ida had become the mother she never had, and so much more. It had been strange to learn there was nothing at all wrong with the older woman, she was experiencing her long time lover's final moments, proof positive of their forbidden love. Georgie had been terrified Ida was dying and leaving her to face the future all alone. It was a shamefully selfish thing to think about, but ultimately, Branford's support had been on account of his son. Who else could understand her situation so well? Branford's passing had killed Ida a little.

Georgie and Ida had been delegated to the balcony seats with the rest of the colored populace who wanted to pay their respects. Lily Anne had sat up front, right next to the coffin of the man who was never really her husband, as dry- eyed and stern faced as ever. The French woman sat beside her, crying prettily into her handkerchief. Beau had not sat with them. He had stood next to where his father rested, his jaw set in a hard, determined line. Georgie could almost see the wheels in his mind working, making plans for heaven knows what. Now she knew. After laying his father into the ground, Beau had gone into the big house for a final time. He had returned to the house he insisted on sharing with her less than a mile away from where his wife resided with his mother, and told her they were all moving to Hawaii, an American territory in the South Pacific. She'd been shocked into to silence, which thinking back was probably a mistake. He hadn't waited for her to find her tongue, just went around packing and giving instructions.

"Wool gathering?"

Georgie jumped at Beau's amused voice. How much like the old Beau he seemed, yet again, he was far more world weary than before. He had grown up so much in such a short time, but then so had she. His smile could still melt her heart, but there was a sad knowledge in those eyes. That young, carefree man Georgie had grown to love was gone forever.

"I still can't believe I'm here," she said by way of explanation. That was all he needed to know. She wasn't about to admit she was weakening, that her heart had already forgiven him no matter what her brain told her.

"I have a surprise for you waiting at the house." Beau smiled that wicked, crooked twist of his generous lips, his eyes sparkling with mischief.

There was a ghost of the Beau she used to know. It made her glad to see something of the playfulness in him. It had been so long since they'd been playful. There was something more about him she was beginning to notice. He seemed much more self-assured. He was more relaxed than he'd been recently. It was almost as if his father's passing had freed him in some unknown way.

"Beau…" It was really useless to try to talk him out of living together. He wouldn't listen no matter how hard she tried. As she suspected, he cut her off.

"Not now, just wait."

What was the use? Sooner or later, she was going to wind up right back where they left off. She knew that. She would fight it with every fiber of her being, but in the end, she couldn't fight the irresistible force that drew her to him. A part of her wanted to be strong enough to tell Beau no, to leave and never look back; but Georgie knew she wouldn't do that. Through all of the mess that had happened, she could never love anyone the way she loved him. No one would ever make her *feel* the way he could, the way he did. Everything about this new Beau intrigued her.

For one thing, he loved Little Beau to distraction. Unlike his father who never acknowledged the children he had with Ida, Beau spent every free minute being a father to his son. He never denied him; in fact, he dared anyone to say anything as he boldly strutted down the streets of Blakely and New Orleans carrying his child. He seemed completely oblivious to the evil eyes of society matrons or the outright astonishment of others. Or maybe he had seen the looks and just didn't care. He seemed to care less and less about rules of polite society.

He had taken his father's empire with both hands and had begun to run it with ruthless efficiency, moving the headquarters here to Hawaii where he would also be instructing brand new Navy pilots part time. Many of Branford's friends and business associates had gone so far as to remove him from various boards of his father's companies. Beau had met the challenge head on, out maneuvering many, and ruthlessly crushing the rest. She would have been concerned at the coldness he exhibited to others, but he never turned that unfeeling ruthlessness toward her, Little Beau, or even Ida.

This new Beau was a man to be reckoned with, and Georgie wasn't sure she was up to the task.

Instead of obsessing over what to do about Beau, Georgie focused on her new surroundings on the drive to wherever they were going. There had been two cars to meet them on arrival. Ida rode with Little Beau in the car ahead of them; Georgie just didn't have the energy to argue about it. Instead, she stared silently out of the window of the sleek black sedan. Beau sat silently by her side, not pressing her, but she could tell he was watching her. She could feel his eyes on her just as surely as if it were his hands caressing her skin.

Pure need coiled in her belly, making her press her legs together in desperate search for relief. There would not be any forthcoming. She knew from experience there was no relief from the gnawing hunger Beau inspired. Just a waning emptiness no one else could fill. Despite the hurt, the pain, the betrayal, every nerve in her body responded to his very presence. Time hadn't lessened her desire for him, it intensified with each passing day, especially since the only times he had been away from her were very brief periods when he flew to the nation's capitol, then here to Hawaii to make preparations. During those times, she couldn't sleep knowing he was away. She could do nothing to stop her heart from yearning for the mere sight of him.

Stop, Georgie. Just stop! She ordered herself.

Concentrating anew, she focused on the passing scenery. Rolling down the window, she felt the wind stroking her face. The air here was in many ways just as thick and sultry as Georgia on a summer day. The scents that the air carried were lighter though, far more exotic. There was a headiness to the smells she couldn't place, but it lightened her heart. The light breeze also brought the slight tang of salt water, cooling what could have been oppressive heat.

It was almost like Georgie had stepped off the plane and on top of a completely different universe. Tall strangely shaped trees danced in the breeze. It seemed unreal such thin trunks could support the fan appendages that were both the branches and the leaves. The landscape was dressed in deep emerald, forest, lime, and deep jades, liberally decorated with blinding bright red, orange, yellow, purple, and pink flowers. It was so beautiful it took her breath away.

"It's beautiful, isn't it?"

Georgie gasped at the deep resonance of his voice. The landscape was a perfect background for her Beau, so much more so than the slow, sweet gentility of the Deep South. Wild and beautiful, and so breathtaking it made a girl weep from the sheer magnitude of the beauty of it; that was Beau, and that was this strange and beautiful land he had brought her to. Everything about this weird and wonderful new place seemed so free and open. The land laid bare its beauty unashamedly, as if daring mere mortals to find fault in the vivid azure sky or gaily decorated foliage. She felt as if the entire island was opening up its arms to her, whispering, "*Welcome home,*" just to her. Just like Beau wanted to welcome her back home in his own arms. Even the birds seemed to be singing, "*Finally a home for Georgie.*" A place she could fit in.

She nodded absently at his comment, not daring to turn around to look at what she knew she would see. Need. Deep, dark, carnal promise glittering in those indigo eyes. His voice spoke volumes, laying bare what he had kept in check for the five months he had been back. So far, he had not pressed her, not since Ida collapsed in New Orleans, but she was constantly aware of his eyes sliding across the curves of her body. She knew his hands were often clenched against the burning desire to reach out and touch. She knew the most male part of his anatomy was constantly hard as steel whenever he watched her with predatory intensity. She knew all this because she felt it too.

All too soon, the drive was over. Not far from the isolated airfield where they had landed, she caught sight of a large salmon colored structure rising up from the lush green backdrop. It was bigger than Beau's home back in Blakely, with a wraparound porch on both floors. A small army of about ten very tall people lined up in the front dressed in what appeared to be brightly decorated sheets.

Georgie's eyes snapped to Beau, who for the first time seemed to be studiously avoiding her direct gaze.

"This is the island of Oahu," Beau informed her, looking toward the house. He was trying to avoid the subject of living arrangements.

He really didn't need to bother. She had no idea what to say exactly. She knew damned well there was nothing she could do short of leaving to dissuade him from his dogged insistence they live together. Despite his mother and his wife knowing she was back in Blakely, he had slept in their former love nest every night. Not in the same bedroom. He would not push her that far, but he had been there with her. On some level, although he had avoided every question she had about the living arrangements, she had known he had planned on it being together. She just never expected he would do so on such a large scale.

"The base is on the other side of the island. I had the airfield built so that I can fly there on the days I need to," he went on in a rush. Funny, he seemed nervous, which was completely contrary to the Beau that had emerged from Branford's funeral. "It shouldn't be more than two or three times a week. It's quicker than driving."

Georgie froze in a mixture of sheer terror and disbelief as the car crawled to a stop. Surely, he didn't mean to parade his mistress in front of what apparently was the household staff. She noted Ida had not emerged from her car either.

"Beau, please no." her plea was little more than a broken whisper. She didn't think she could stand it. It was humiliating enough being the other woman, which was most assuredly her destiny.

"Georgie, look at me sugar."

She didn't want to, but she was helpless not to respond to the quiet authority of his voice. Her eyes, shimmering with unshed tears sought his, trying desperately to hold on to the thin thread of her composure.

"Trust in me," although his tone was sure and confident, there was an underlying entreaty. "This one last time, please trust in me."

There was no reason to, really. He had not given her any cause to trust him. Not in something like this. Still, her heart overruled her head. As much as she wanted to yell and scream, and strike out, she couldn't. She was so damn raw. She didn't think she could survive another disloyalty. Yet, she allowed him to take her hand and lead her out of the car.

Georgie walked as if in a daze over to collect Ida and the baby. Her heart banged so hard against her ribcage, it hurt to draw in each breath. The roar of her blood rushing through her veins was so loud she couldn't really hear her introduction to the massive woman with skin the color of peaches and gold. She had the features of a mulatto—sort of—with a thick wreath of jet-black hair laced with white strands piled high on her head. She was wrapped in a ruby cloth decorated with pristine white flowers. She blinked dumbly as the woman addressed her, but surely she must have heard wrong.

"Mrs. Dupuis?"

She shook her head in denial even as Beau silently nudged her.

Why would he do that? Why would he tell these people she was his wife? Her face burned with the horror. Why?

"Hang on, baby," Beau whispered in her ear. "Just hang on."

The woman went through introductions of the household staff in some kind of bizarre turn of the century ritual. She felt uncomfortable in her own skin. It just seemed so off, so wrong.

"Would you like a tour of the house?"

What was the woman's name? Lana? Luana?

"I think we would just like to rest for a bit," Beau answered for her.

"I will show you to your room then," the woman chirped on brightly.

How obscene for the mysterious mammoth woman to be so cheerful when Georgie felt so sick to her very soul. She would not pretend to be something she wasn't. Something she had no hopes of being. It hurt too much. She knew the truth, she would always know who and what she really was.

She allowed Beau to drag her along, dreading what confrontation they had to have. He could either build her a smaller home somewhere close, or stash her away in the nearest town, but she would not be staying here.

"The room was finished just as you instructed," the woman told Beau. Her voice was really quite beautiful in spite of the macabre scene they were playing out. The only one knowing the rules seemed to be Beau.

Beau, the man who had managed to break her heart yet again. She was going to have to leave him for good. He would just keep doing it, unintentionally, but thoroughly stabbing her heart and stomping it to pieces.

"You rest now," the woman stopped outside the double doors on the far side of the bottom floor. Ida and Little Beau had been taken upstairs, a pair of very tall, statuesque giggling young women cooing over her child. She would gather them later, after she dealt with Beau.

She allowed Beau to lead her inside the room, closing her eyes as she heard to the click of the lock of the door, imaging it was a lock on her heart, wishing with all her heart it could be so easy as to lock the man behind her out of her life for good.

Taking a deep breath, Georgie gathered what remained of her once again shattered pride to face her future.

Chapter Fourteen

Beau could feel the storm brewing underneath the surface. Georgie's pain slashed at him just as surely as it slashed her. He knew what she was thinking, what she was feeling. He had no one to blame but himself that she couldn't trust him to make it right. And he was going to make it right. He had been the driving force behind his every action for the past three months. His son was attempting to walk, and he was saying simply words like "Mama" and "Dada." He would grow up addressing him as Daddy, and he would be just that.

"Don't," Beau cut off the thunder before it began. "Turn around, Georgie."

"I can't-I won't…"

"Damn it, Georgie, just turn around!"

He hadn't meant to yell, but he was far more afraid than he had ever been in his life. If she walked away now, there was really nothing left for him.

With an icy glare meant to express to him all the anger she was feeling, she turned on her heel and gasped. She was so still, he was beginning to wonder about the wisdom of his plan.

Would she reject him outright? Would she slap him, scream, holler, call him everything but a son of God?

He was close to breaking down himself before she finally moved toward the ivory gown draped on the bed.

"What…what is this?"

Her fingers shook as she reached out to trail her slim, dainty fingers along the inlaid pearls.

"What do you think it is?"

He knew he shouldn't be teasing, but he was inordinately drawn by the wonder on her face. Her eyes were wide, almost swallowing her pixie like face. Her smooth, flawless skin notably flushed despite her naturally dark tone. The hope behind those liquid brown pools was heartbreaking. His only goal was to fulfill the hope, to satisfy her deepest desire.

"Beau?"

A lone tear trailed down her face as she faced him. Lord, what he wouldn't do for this woman. Right here was the sole reason for his very existence. Just Georgie. Only Georgie.

"Georgina Mae Willard," Beau whispered taking her hand and dropping to one knee. "Would you do me the greatest honor of becoming my wife?" Slipping on the ring that had been weighing down his pocket for the last three months, Beau tried begging with his eyes, willfully projecting all the love he had in his being into one look.

It was not the ring Marie had worn. For all he knew, she might still be wearing the simple band he bought in England.

The ring he slipped on Georgie's finger had been his grandmother's. Branford had never given it to Lily, and there was no way in hell Beau would have ever let it rest on Marie's fingers. This ring had always been meant for Georgie.

"But, Marie…You're married!"

Beau winced at the pain laced in the statement. Damn, maybe he shouldn't have waited until they got here to tell her about the divorce.

"I'm divorced," he told her. "I have the papers if you want to see them."

"When?"

"Right after the funeral. It took longer than my…my father and I had hoped." Branford had worked tirelessly, bribing a bitterly married old judge to grant Beau the divorce. They had had to be careful. No one could know the real reason for his divorce. No one could know that he planned to make Georgie his wife, and no one could know Marie was Jewish. The United States was not taking many Jewish immigrants. Too many had flooded out of Europe as it was. The powers that be were nervous about bigoted constituents.

"Why?"

She had to be kidding! Beau was simply dumfounded. Didn't she know how much he loved her?

Standing to gather her in his arms, Beau lifted her chin to meet his direct gaze. "I love you, Georgie. I would move the heaven and earth if you asked me to. I would kill for you, and I would die for you. There is nothing I wouldn't do to be with you. There is nothing I wouldn't give you. All I ask is that you never leave me. If I make a mistake, tell me and I will make it right. There is nothing, Georgie, I wouldn't do for you."

There was more, but he didn't say it. He didn't say how he wanted to grow old with her, sit out on the porch, and just let the world go by. He didn't say how much he wanted her right now, how he burned for her.

"How can we?" her voice caught as she struggled. She didn't want the dream to end, he could understand that. "I mean, it's not legal-"

"Georgie baby, Hawaii is a territory, not a state. There are no laws against it here."

Georgie stared at him, slack-jawed, but saying nothing. Her eyes were wide and frightened, and more than just a hint of hurt lurked in those beautifully sweet, brown orbs, which glistened with tears as she just stared. Lord, this was not going the way he had planned, but when had anything where Georgie was concerned?

Quickly going over to where their bags had been placed, he threw papers out of his briefcase, looking for his divorce papers.

"Look, baby," he urged, desperate to get her to say something, anything. "Look for yourself. I am divorced…Well, the marriage was annulled really. We never consummated the marriage so..."

He shrugged without going into it. He could tell her he couldn't stand the touch of Marie. No matter how hard Marie had tried, he could never sleep with any woman but Georgie. She was all he ever wanted, all he ever needed. All other women paled in comparison. But then, it had always been only her, from the moment she turned sweet sixteen. He couldn't have her then, so he had waited. One taste and he was a goner.

His father had told him it had been that way with Ida. That he had never wanted another woman, but one drunken night at a house party had sealed his fate forever. That was why Branford had worked so damn hard to get Beau out of his disastrous marriage. While his father insisted he had never regretted his birth, Beau knew he regretted the hell out of not being able to run away with Ida like he had planned before Lily Anne, and Beau's mother had known that. She had known it and had resented the hell out of that fact.

Beau could not blame his mother for being resentful, but she was far from the innocent victim. She had trapped Branford into marriage, and she had done a million and one things over the years to make his life hell. She had not been able get back at Ida for stealing the love of man who never wanted her in the first place. Branford would have killed her with his bare hands, or worse, left her. But she could, and did, make Branford pay.

When Beau had brought Georgie to the house Branford had provided for the lovebirds, Lily had lost what fragile hold she had on her sanity. Always cold and calculating, the woman had become positively homicidal.

"You never slept with your wife?"

Georgie's incredulous questions snapped Beau back to the here and now.

"How could I?" he asked with honest anguish. "All I have ever wanted was you."

Falling to his knees in front of the woman he loved with every fiber of his being, he rested his head on her stomach pulling her close.

"I am so sorry, baby. I never meant to hurt you. I didn't know what to do." To hell with being the man. He let the tears he had held back for so long flow down his cheeks. He couldn't lose her now. "There is no excuse for what I did-"

"Yes, there is."

Half-afraid he hadn't heard her right, he rocked back on his heels, staring up at the woman he wanted to make his permanently and legally more than anything else in the world.

"What did you say?"

He prayed he had heard her correctly. He was terrified of the answer, but he had to know.

Georgie sighed, burying her fingers into his hair. A tortured moan escaped his lips as he leaned into her touch. It felt so damn good. He had been so afraid he would never feel her touch of her own free will ever again.

"She saved your life."

It cost her, that small confession that she understood why he married another, ripping her heart into shreds. He knew it did.

Standing slowly, he gathered her in his arms, more grateful than he had ever been in his life she didn't pull away, but sank into his embrace.

"I hurt you." Such a pitiful thing to say now, but it was all he could think of.

"Beau, you did the only thing you knew to do." Admitting it to herself hurt. Georgie had used her anger to ease her pain. It hadn't worked completely, but it had worked enough to allow her to keep her sanity. Now was the time to stop the hurt. He had done so much to attempt to make up for something he had felt he had to do.

It didn't change the many months she had been in agony; first, wondering if he was still alive, terrified she would never see him again, never know about the beautiful son their love had created. Then, having him return with a wife in tow. The last part had damned near killed her inside. But all along, she had known.

Beau loved her. He had always loved her. He had gone about getting her in all the wrong ways, but he loved her. She hadn't doubted it for some time now. She knew in the deepest corner of her heart that he would not leave her or Little Beau ever again. She knew he had learned a hard lesson over in Europe. He was not invincible, he didn't have all the answers, and his reckless behavior had very real consequences to people other than himself. To go on punishing him when it was killing them both was as senseless as it was useless, and she was damned tired of making him pay, only to make herself hurt worse. In the end, hurting him only hurt her more, and she was tired of the hurt.

"You haven't been with anyone?" she had to know. He may not have slept with Marie, but Beau was a highly sensual man.

"I couldn't do that to you too. Marrying was bad enough."

Georgie rose on her toes to place a soft kiss on his lips. She had intended for the kiss to be soft anyway.

As soon as their lips touched, the irresistible desire that pulled them together with intensely magnetic force would not allow either of them to pull away. Soft kisses of reunion grew into full-blown passion that had lain dormant for far too long. Beau's tongue invaded the sweet cavern of her mouth cautiously at first, quickly becoming the dominant conqueror he was naturally. He left no part of her mouth unexplored, reacquainting himself with every nook and cranny.

Georgie moaned into his mouth as he drew her closer, leaving not an inch of daylight between them. His strong hands gripped her buttocks, lifting her to grind against the hard shaft in his pants.

Oh, how she had missed this! She missed his expert mastery over her body, over her very senses. She lifted her leg, trying to get closer. She needed Beau like she needed air. It had been far too long, and her body ached for him.

"Georgie, sugar, we have to stop," Beau groaned against the side of her neck.

"I don't want to stop," she pouted, angling her head to give him better access to the sensitive skin of her neck. "I missed you so much!"

"I missed you too, sugar. Never doubt that. But this is not going to happen until you are my wife."

"You really mean that, don't you?"

For as long as she had wanted this very thing, a respectable marriage, Georgie found that she was suddenly petrified at the prospect actually getting married.

"I couldn't be more serious," he replied forcefully, pushing away ever so slightly. He was doggedly determined to do it right this time.

"I don't want to wait," Georgie whimpered, trying to get him close once more.

"I mean it, Georgie. I want…I need to do this right."

Georgie pouted, her delectably pouty bottom lip sticking out so cutely.

So, before she could try and continue arguing with him, he cut off the argument he knew was coming.

"You better hurry and get dressed; the preacher is waiting for us."

The sooner she was safely Mr. Beau Cantwell Dupuis, the sooner they could take this back to the bedroom, the better.

In the meantime, he had to get his wife to the altar.

Chapter Fifteen

Looking down at the wedding ring on her finger, Georgie pinched herself to make sure the last two hours didn't fade away. All of her life she had wanted this moment more than anything else in the universe, and now she had it. She had thought this moment was the thing that would complete her the most. Becoming a wife, being respectful, had always seemed to be the pinnacle of all her dreams, and she was there. Finally, she was more than the bastard daughter of a backwoods juke joint owner. She was no longer the Dupuis boy's whore. She was Mrs. Georgiana Dupuis.

Funny, she'd thought the beautiful ceremony in the unbelievably lush and fragrant garden full of color and life, officiated by the rather large yet soft-spoken minister whose hair was longer than any woman Georgie had ever seen, would have been the epitome of all she had ever wished for. Only it wasn't. It was not the words out of the mammoth preacher's mouth that completed her, or even made her happy.

It was the sapphire eyes that beheld her with such wonder she was humbled to her very soul. It was the firm grip on her hand that would not let go, even after they said their vows, and the pronouncement declared they were well and truly married. It was the man who now was holding onto their son as they were being slowly driven back to the massive house near the beach. In her search for the "perfect life," Georgie had almost missed the thing she had needed the most—love.

Thinking back at how close she had come to marrying someone else, or how hard she had fought Beau in the beginning, made her shiver in absolute dread. She had almost let her pride push Beau away permanently, when she had always known the truth. She had known whatever compelled him to marry another woman, knowing she was waiting at home, had to be one hell of a reason. Although he had hurt her, and he should have never flown off to fight for a country that was not his own, he hadn't known about Little Beau. She should have told him. She could have, yet she had kept the knowledge to herself, refusing to use her pregnancy to keep him home.

There were just too many things they both could have, and probably should have, done differently, all water under the bridge now. They were both older and wiser, and maybe this way was best. As for herself, Georgie knew she had a greater appreciation for her life, and for Beau. The rough road had made her stronger, and as much as she loved the man beside her, she knew she would have been okay no matter what had happened.

Yeah, it would have hurt like hell had Beau not been able to divorce, or rather annul his marriage. But she was woman enough to admit that sooner or later, she would have wound up right back in Beau's arms. Her father was right in most of the things he had told her. She was far better knowing love than being in a marriage without one. There were a great many things he had gotten so very wrong, but she would deal with that later.

As Ida rushed to take the baby as they exited the car, Georgie took a deep calming breath. This was it.

"Why don't we share dinner with Ida and Little Beau?" Beau suggested nervously, pulling on the collar of his shirt.

He looked so handsome in his tailored midnight blue suit, and so nervous it threw her for a loop. She could see him being nervous about asking her to marry him, she had been anything but encouraging since he returned from Europe. In fact, she had been downright cold. But when it came to the physical, Beau was anything but shy and retiring.

Placing her hand on his arm, she halted him from going into the house.

"Beau?"

She needed him. She needed him to be inside her, making her whole. It had been so very long, her body hummed with electric anticipation. She ached. She missed his touch so much, she wanted to weep.

Taking a rough breath, Beau looked down upon his entire world. Looking into those eyes he didn't know whether he wanted to dance a jig or fall to his knees in thanksgiving. If she only knew how badly he wanted to rip that flowing white sundress from her body and take her right there. He had been so hard for so long, he knew it would be rough, and she didn't deserve that.

"Sugar, I think we need to take this slow." He blew out another breath, running a distracted hand through his hair while keeping her smaller hand firmly in the grip of the other. He couldn't seem to let her go, not after coming so close to losing her forever. How could he explain to her that he was terrified he was going to fall all over her like a mad man? "I don't think I can be that...gentle."

He had spent months upon months dreaming about this woman. She was the first thing he thought about in the morning and his last thought every night. He was a grown man, yet he wanted to weep like a baby when he thought of the curves he knew were underneath that dress.

"I never asked you to be gentle, Beau."

Damn. It was hell holding it together, and she wasn't making it any easier. He was about a heartbeat away from throwing her over his shoulder.

"Georgie, I don't think you understand..."

"Do you really think I don't need you just as bad?" she cut in. "Do you think I don't burn every bit as much? That my body isn't calling for you?" Lifting their entwined hands, she placed his hand on her chest, right above her breast. His hands itched on contact. So damn close. "I need you, Beau. I don't want to wait."

That was it. Sweeping her in his arms, he half ran into the house, not pausing until he entered the bedroom, slamming the door with his foot. Placing Georgie on her feet next to the bed, his hands shook as he moved to remove the white silk from her body. Every inch of bare skin revealed only added fuel to his already raging fire. He stopped to kiss as much of the smooth flesh exposed as he slid the dress down her luscious body. She seemed more generously curved than she had been before, making him even hotter as he laid her down to allow his hands and lips to travel everywhere. He was so damn hard he was dizzy with it. Once would not be enough tonight.

Avoiding the small hands tugging at his clothing, he kissed her lips as if he wasn't about to die if he wasn't buried inside her soon. He took his time, working her up to a frenzy. Georgie loved deep, sensual kisses. He missed giving them to her.

"Beau! I need you now! Please?"

They were the most beautiful words ever spoken, expanding his heart so full it would surely burst.

"Shhh, baby. Let me love you," he murmured against the silk of her skin.

He had to taste all of her. He needed the taste of her on his tongue. Working his lips to her breast, he suckled each mound with infinite care and attention, lightly biting each nipple until it pebbled rock hard in his mouth. Her breasts were most definitely larger, heavier. Although she had ceased breastfeeding, they had lost none of the ripe fullness. He wished he could spend all night loving them, but there was so much more he needed to show equal attention.

Traveling lower, he spent a few moments dipping his tongue into her navel. It was one of her hot spots; it never failed to make her arch into his embrace. Today was no different.

"Beau!" she gasped, tugging at his hair. Damn he missed that. "Please! Stop teasing!"

He had to smile as he ran his mouth slowly southward. She had no idea. This was driving him insane every bit as much as he was making her. But he needed this. He needed to get reacquainted with every inch of her body. It was like coming home after too long away. He wanted everything.

Finally reaching his destination, he held her thighs open as he simply inhaled her scent.

Mine! Every fiber of his being screamed it. Finally, finally.

At the first lazy stroke of his tongue, Georgie let loose a guttural moan and sank down on the bed. So good! It felt so unbelievably, fantastically good. She could not imagine any other man where Beau was now, between her wantonly spread thighs, lavishing soul-shattering attention at her very core. His tongue took several long licks before plunging inside. A few thrusts, then he moved upward to suckle her pleasure button, making her hips buck in response.

"YES!" the scream tore through her as she crashed into a mind numbing orgasm. "Oh, Beau! I missed you so much!"

His only response was to moan against her flooding pussy, licking up every drop he could. He was far from done, she knew. Beau had always loved being exactly where he was right now. True to form, he continued the expert torture, alternating between making love to her with his tongue, parrying and thrusting until she was seeing stars, then suckling, licking, even lightly biting her clit. He drove her to orgasm after orgasm until she couldn't remember her name. Just when she thought she might go insane from the blinding pleasure, he rose to stare down at her.

When had removed his clothes? His body was gloriously bare, exposed for her perusal. In a daze, she reached out to touch the hard planes of his chest, running her hands over his scorching skin. Without realizing what she was doing, she placed her mouth on each nipple, then pulling each slightly with her teeth.

"Damn, Georgie!" Beau moaned, entwining his hand in her hair.

Oh, how he missed her touch! He had to tug on her hair to stop her from dipping lower. There was no way he would ever last if he allowed her to put her mouth anywhere near his cock. He needed to be inside her.

He urged her down to lie on her back, holding her legs open so he could slide home. A long hiss escaped his lips as he worked his way inside. She was tight, so excruciatingly tight, it took everything in him to be patient, slowly working his way inside instead of thrusting forward as he desperately wanted to do. Mewing whimpers emanated from Georgie as filled her. Although she was dripping wet, he had to take shallow strokes, allowing her to adjust as he moved forward.

For Georgie, he was moving too slow. Her hips rose insistently, trying to force him all the way in.

"Baby, you are so tight! I don't want to hurt you."

She didn't listen. She slammed her hips up once more, jamming every inch of him deep inside.

"Shit!"

She was blistering hot! Had it always felt this good? He gulped in air, closing his eyes in an attempt to stay in control. It wasn't working, not with the woman beneath him squirming around his cock trying to get him to move. His hips responded of their own accord, sliding out so far only the throbbing head of his penis remained, them plunging down until their pelvises mashed together.

"You feel so damn good wrapped around my dick, baby," he groaned, never stopping the pounding rhythm. "That's right, sweetheart. Move with me."

Georgie couldn't remember feeling so full, so complete. Each thrust drove her higher and higher. The edge of pain brought sweet, sensual pleasure so intense, she couldn't form words, only gasp and cry out in pure ecstasy. Her legs wrapped around Beau, trying to force him even deeper into her womb. It wasn't enough! She needed more.

The dirty words whispered urgently in her ear added to the explosive passion. She loved it when he did that, and he remembered.

"Do you know how much I missed my pussy?" he demanded. "Mine! All mine."

And she was. Completely and utterly, she belonged to his man, and he was most definitely taking possession of all that was his. Her body ebbed and flowed with his, both of their movements becoming fast and furious. Her fingers dug into his shoulders, anchoring her against the storm.

"Good. So good." It was a prayer and a fact.

She came so many times, her eyes crossed, her throat raw from the screams he inspired.

"Fuck, Georgie, I'm going to come!"

So was she—again.

As he exploded inside her, Georgie imploded, coming completely apart with a scream.

Although he had come, Beau didn't stop. He couldn't. He was still rock hard, and there was nothing in the world that could stop him from driving inside her.

"I can't stop, baby. I need you so bad."

"Take me, Beau," came the whispered reply that sent him flying. "Never stop."

And he didn't until the first orange lights of dawn.

Coming Soon...

Loving Georgie

"I don't believe we've been introduced." He wasn't going to answer him until he knew who the hell he was. The cocky grin that graced the man's face didn't ease his discomfort any, especially since the grin didn't meet his eyes. Eyes that seemed to be taking in a lot more than the scenery.

"Leslie Reiling, Office of Strategic Services."

"Shit." Beau didn't want to hear anymore but short of jumping out of the jeep, there was little he could do to stop the words he knew were coming. "No. I'll fly a damn plan. I will join the fucking Navy, but there is no way in hell I'm going to be a spook."

"Well, now that's fine," the man, Leslie suddenly developed a southern accent as deep as his own. It sounded so authentic Beau had no idea whether or not it was real or if he was playing head games. "Asking you was more of a courtesy, your knowledge of French Underground members aside. What we really need is your wife."